# WINE COUNTRY COURIER
*Community Buzz*

Well, it seems anyone who is anyone was in attendance at the Candle-lighters Bachelorette Auction at the Ashton Estate Winery—at least 450 somebodies of the social elite were there. And boy, did they raise some money. One adorable bachelorette was sold for an impressive $10,000! That is one expensive date. I just hope the sophisticated Miss Paige Ashton knows how to swim, considering the shark that bid the highest. I'm talking about one Walker Camberlane. Sure, he's handsome and charming and incredibly irresistible, but he's never been known to s down, and he's sure to take Miss Ashton for a walk on the wild side. Talk about complete opposites!

And still the investigation surrounding Spencer Ashton's murder continues. When in the world are we going to get some answers? Rumor is the police are getting closer to the truth and they seem to have some secret piece of evidence that they will be sharing with the families. This reporter is waiting with bated breath for a resolution.

Dear Reader,

Sit back, relax and indulge yourself with all the fabulous offerings from Silhouette Desire this October. Roxanne St. Claire is penning the latest DYNASTIES: THE ASHTONS with *The Highest Bidder*. Youngest Ashton sibling, Paige, finds herself participating in a bachelorette auction and being "won" by a sexy stranger. Strangers also make great protectors, as demonstrated by Annette Broadrick in *Danger Becomes You*, her most recent CRENSHAWS OF TEXAS title.

Speaking of protectors, Michelle Celmer's heroine in *Round-the-Clock Temptation* gets a bodyguard of her very own: a member of the TEXAS CATTLEMAN'S CLUB. Linda Conrad wraps up her miniseries THE GYPSY INHERITANCE with *A Scandalous Melody*. Will this mysterious music box bring together two lonely hearts? For something a little darker, why not try *Secret Nights at Nine Oaks* by Amy J. Fetzer? A handsome recluse, an antebellum mansion—two great reasons to stay indoors. And be sure to catch Heidi Betts's *When the Lights Go Down*, the story of a plain-Jane librarian out to make some serious changes in her humdrum love life.

As you can see, Silhouette Desire has lots of great stories for you to enjoy. So spend this first month of autumn cuddled up with a good book—and come back next month for even more fabulous reads.

Enjoy!

*Melissa Jeglinski*

Melissa Jeglinski
Senior Editor
Silhouette Desire

Please address questions and book requests to:
Silhouette Reader Service
U.S.: 3010 Walden Ave., P.O. Box 1325, Buffalo, NY 14269
Canadian: P.O. Box 609, Fort Erie, Ont. L2A 5X3

# THE HIGHEST BIDDER

## Roxanne St. Claire

Published by Silhouette Books
**America's Publisher of Contemporary Romance**

Special thanks and acknowledgment are given to
Roxanne St. Claire for her contribution to the
DYNASTIES: THE ASHTONS series.

This one's for the Space Coast Authors of Romance…
the brightest stars in my writing world!

 **SILHOUETTE BOOKS**

ISBN 0-373-76681-5

THE HIGHEST BIDDER

**Books by Roxanne St. Claire**

Silhouette Desire

*Like a Hurricane* #1572
*A Fire Still Burns* #1608
*When the Earth Moves* #1648
*The Highest Bidder* #1681

---

## ROXANNE ST. CLAIRE

began writing romance fiction in 1999 after nearly two decades as a public relations and marketing executive. Retiring from business to pursue a lifelong dream of writing romance is one of the most rewarding accomplishments in her life. The others are her happy marriage to a real-life hero and the daily joys of raising two young children. Roxanne writes mainstream romantic suspense, contemporary romance and women's fiction. Her work has received numerous awards, including the prestigious Heart to Heart Award, the Golden Opportunity Award and the Gateway Award. An active member of the Romance Writers of America, Roxanne lives in Florida and currently writes—and raises children—full-time. She loves to hear from readers through e-mail at roxannestc@aol.com and snail mail at P.O. Box 372909, Satellite Beach, FL 32937. Visit her Web site at www.roxannestclaire.com.

# THE ASHTONS

Frederick Ashton m Patricia Winston

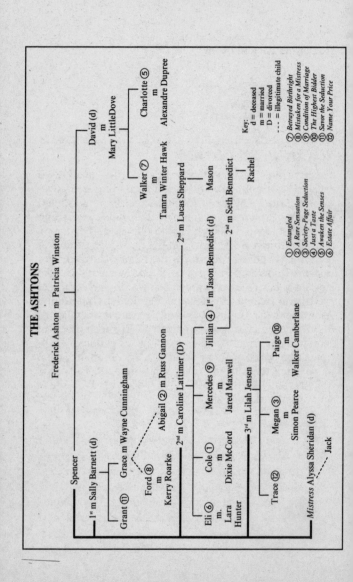

**Key:**
d = deceased
m = married
D = divorced
--- = illegitimate child

① Entangled
② A Rare Sensation
③ Society-Page Seduction
④ Just a Taste
⑤ Awaken the Senses
⑥ Estate Affair
⑦ Betrayed Birthright
⑧ Mistaken for a Mistress
⑨ Condition of Marriage
⑩ The Highest Bidder
⑪ Savor the Seduction
⑫ Name Your Price

Spencer

1st m Sally Barnett (d)

Grant ⑪
m
Kerry Roarke

Grace m Wayne Cunningham

Abigail ② m Russ Gannon

Ford ⑧
m
Kerry Roarke

David (d)
m
Mary LittleDove

Walker ⑦
m
Tamra Winter Hawk

Charlotte ⑤
m
Alexandre Dupree

2nd m Lucas Sheppard

Mason

2nd m Caroline Lattimer (D)

Mercedes ⑨
m
Jared Maxwell

Jillian ④ 1st m Jason Bennedict (d)

2nd m Seth Bennedict

Rachel

Eli ⑥
m.
Lara
Hunter

Cole ①
m
Dixie McCord

3rd m Lilah Jensen

Paige ⑩
m
Walker Camberlane

Trace ⑫

Megan ③
m
Simon Pearce

Mistress Alyssa Sheridan (d)

Jack

# Prologue

**S**pencer Ashton studied the inviting sway of the woman's hips as she sashayed across his spacious office and out the door, ending the interview but starting the mating dance.

His choice was made. This one was young, eager and ambitious enough to request a fancy title—"administrative assistant." With an amused snort, he spun his chair around to the fog-tipped view of San Francisco eighteen floors below.

A little ambition in a secretary was good, he thought wryly. Then they understand just what they have to give in order to get. Too much ambition, on the other hand, and they cease to be satisfied with promises and pay raises, and the demands get stronger...and turn into ultimatums.

At the thought, the image of his wife appeared in his head. Lilah Jensen had been the perfect secretary—smart and sexy. A breath of fresh air after all those years married to the mouse, Caroline Lattimer. And now, seventeen years and three children later, Lilah was still smart enough to keep her mouth shut and look the other way when she had to. She had the status she craved as Lilah *Ashton,* and he had the freedom he required. Shrewd woman, Lilah. Always was.

This new secretary would be good. She'd flipped her hair and wet her lips enough times to let him know she'd do whatever he asked. He inhaled a satisfied breath, puffing up his chest with a deep breath and liking the way his still-toned muscles stretched the fabric of his custom-made shirt. She couldn't be more than twenty-five, about half his age. With a grin, he patted his hard-muscled stomach. Spencer Ashton still had it all. Good looks, a hard body and more money than God.

His quick laugh at that thought was interrupted by a tap on his door.

"What is it?" he called out, gruffly enough to communicate his distaste at any intrusion that he didn't plan. Whoever it was should be stopped by his secretary and buzzed in through her.

The door inched open and the woman he'd just interviewed gave him a wary look. "Sorry to bother you, Mr. Ashton. Just one more thing."

Damn, she hadn't even started yet. He swallowed the reprimand and flashed an easy smile. "You're no bother…" Donna? Debbie? He couldn't remember.

"I was just in the reception area and, uh, I noticed your secretary, well, she sort of packed up her bag and left."

The little bitch. She'd figured out that the string of women he'd been interviewing were her potential replacements, before he had a chance to give her enough severance pay to guarantee silence. He cursed his thoughtless mistake.

His gaze swept over the brunette in front of him, making no effort to hide his admiration. "Then I hope you can start tomorrow."

She did the hair toss again, and her eyes sparkled. She might as well have rubbed her crotch. The message was the same.

"I can start right now, Mr. Ashton," she replied in a low voice.

He felt himself respond. "Good."

"As a matter of fact," she took a few more steps into the room and held out a thin white envelope. "While I was out there, a messenger delivered this for you. It says personal and confidential, so I didn't open it."

He nodded and absently took the envelope, his attention still on the generous rise of her breasts she'd thoughtfully revealed by removing her jacket. "Thank you."

"I'll just get settled at the desk," she added with a smile. "And thank *you*."

She turned to leave, offering him that nice backside view again. "Just a second…" Dorie? Damn, what was her name?

"Yes, sir?"

"You may have to work a little late tonight." He gave her an appropriately innocent look. "Just to learn some of the Ashton-Lattimer policies and procedures."

"No problem, Mr. Ashton."

He dropped the letter on the vast, empty surface of his desk and picked up his phone to call Lilah to let her know he'd be staying in his city apartment tonight and not driving home as he'd planned.

As he dialed the private line to his estate winery in

Napa, his gaze fell on the envelope. On the front, his name was typed, with no return address.

While the phone rang in his ear, he sliced the envelope with his finger and swore as the paper cut a quarter-inch slash in his skin. He'd have to train... whatever the hell her name was...to open everything for him.

"Ashton Estate."

He recognized the voice of his housekeeper, Irena, and didn't bother with pleasantries. "Give me Lilah."

"Of course, Mr. Ashton. One moment, please."

As he waited for his wife, he sucked the drop of blood from his finger and pulled out a folded sheet of paper from the envelope. When he opened it, a yellowed newspaper clipping fluttered onto the desk. What the hell was this?

Like the envelope, the note was typed. One paragraph. No date. No signature.

An unholy tendril of apprehension snaked through him as he read the first sentence, the cut finger still in his mouth.

"Bigamy is against the law."

He swallowed and tasted the bitterness of his own blood as he read:

Enclosed is the obituary of one Sally Barnett Ashton. Unfortunately, this newspaper seems to be in error. In the third paragraph it states that Mrs. Sally Barnett Ashton was divorced from her husband, Spencer Ashton, at the time of her death. In fact, Mrs. Sally Barnett Ashton was never divorced. Careful research reveals no divorce documents to be found in Crawley, Nebraska, or San Francisco, California. According to the laws of both states, that means her husband couldn't re-marry as long as Mrs. Sally Barnett Ashton re-mained alive. If he did, such a union would be illegal, and any results of that union would be null and void. Wouldn't the second Mrs. Ashton be interested to learn that her marriage—and the subsequent divorce settlement—was not legal?

The taste in his mouth turned metallic, as white-hot anger shot through his veins.

He picked up the clipping and stared at the obituary of the woman he'd been forced to marry thirty years ago. His gaze dropped to the handwritten note in the newspaper margin.

"It'd be a damn shame for anyone to find out about this."

His fists balled as tightly as the knot in his gut. No one would blackmail Spencer Ashton. No one would dare. He'd kill them with his bare hands first.

"Hello, darling." Lilah trilled in his ear. "Sorry to keep you holding. Don't tell me you're not coming home."

Disgust and something frighteningly close to fear strained his chest. "Of course I am." He glanced at his closed office door and thought of the new secretary. There'd be plenty of time for that. He needed to think tonight. "I'm leaving here around six."

"Wonderful, darling. Then you haven't forgotten it's Paige's birthday. The party is Saturday, but your baby is ten today."

"Of course I haven't forgotten."

He hung up without another word and grabbed the letter again, watching in horror as a single drop of his blood spread a scarlet stain on the paper.

Swearing, he tore the sheet in half again and again until he had dozens of pieces in his hand. Then he stuffed them all into the trash.

# One

"**A**nd the lady is…sold! To the gentleman at table four!"

The auctioneer's gavel smacked the podium and the 450 guests in the Ashton Estate Winery reception hall erupted in a chorus of cheers and boos. The bidding for a date with the blond Napa Valley socialite, also known as bachelorette number seventeen, had been fast and furious.

She had a name—the auctioneer had even said it—but Paige Ashton's mind worked better with numbers than names. And now that number seventeen was bought and paid for, there were only three women left before dessert and dancing could commence. Then Paige was done.

She hugged her clipboard and beamed from the side of the stage. They were just shy of the magic number of $20,000, to be raised for the Candlelighters of Northern California. God bless the brave ladies willing to parade on that stage, willing to let men shout out dollar amounts they'd pay for a date.

Not only was it a wonderful cause, the annual Candlelighters Bachelorette Auction was a smashing event, and she'd coordinated every detail for the "Take a Walk on the Wild Side" jungle theme right down to rainforest-inspired centerpieces. It had been a breeze after the balancing act she'd been performing with her family the past few months.

Still, she'd been a little nervous about executing this event—her first on her own since she'd returned home to the winery to help her sister handle the massive functions held at the world-famous estate. Megan would be proud, if she weren't in the throes of morning sickness. Paige planned to debrief her sister on the success the next day, and they'd share a welcome reprieve from discussing their father's murder and the various leads the police were following to find the person who shot Spencer Ashton.

"Tiffany Valencia is gone."

The words, whispered to Paige by one of the auction aides, tickled her ear and raised a hair on the back of her neck.

"Gone? Number eighteen is gone?" It didn't take her lightning-speed brain to solve this problem. "Get nineteen."

The aide, a young intern for the auction company, shook her head. "No can do. That one just left with Ashley Bleeker for a smoke."

"Bleeker? That means eighteen, nineteen *and* twenty are gone?"

"We have to take a break."

"No break," Paige insisted. That would ruin the

rhythm of the event and, worse, stop the bidding. The event would ultimately be judged by how much money was raised. "Where the heck is eighteen—er, Tiffany?"

"I think she met a guy and took off with him," the aide said apologetically.

Paige rolled her eyes. "He's supposed to *pay* for that privilege."

The aide shrugged and looked up at the stage where the auctioneer was peering at them. "You better tell George. He's not good at ad-libbing. He needs someone to auction off."

Paige didn't waste a moment thinking about what needed to be done. "Get the band in place, we're almost done with the auction portion. Let me talk to George and see if he can keep things moving until we find her." She gave the aide her clipboard and took a deep breath, her palms suddenly too damp to risk smoothing her silk skirt.

How did these girls do it? Just going onstage to chat with the auctioneer raised her heart rate.

The room quieted a little as she stepped into the spotlights that flooded the stage. Someone whistled from the back.

Good heavens. They thought she was the next bachelorette. Paige threw an apologetic smile into the crowd and shook her head, but the lights blinded her. She could only make out a few faces in the very front, one of them her cousin Walker, looking both surprised and amused.

"Well, here's a shocker!" The auctioneer further hushed the crowd with his booming voice. "Paige Ashton is bachelorette number eighteen."

Blood drained from her head and rushed to her pounding heart. "No, no, I'm not." Her denial was too soft to be heard over the rowdy response. She'd done her job and made sure the Ashton wine flowed freely. Now she had a roomful of inebriated men who'd have applauded *any* female at this point.

"I don't have a fact sheet on Paige," the auctioneer admitted, his commanding voice hardly needing a microphone. "But I know firsthand that she's a delight to work with. She's—how old, Paige?"

"Twenty-two!" She recognized Walker's voice, and one more glance at her cousin revealed his fairly evil grin. He leaned over to say something to another man, missing the dirty look Paige directed at their table.

"How much do we hear for this twenty-two-year-old beauty with a well-known last name and an angel's face?"

Death. Death would be preferable to the lights burning her cheeks—or was that just one massive blush that threatened to explode every blood vessel in her face?

"Five hundred!"

Oh, dear God. They were *bidding*. She held up a hand to stop them, but the auctioneer grabbed it, spinning her in a Fred Astaire-like move. "Just five hundred? Look at this beautiful young lady. Svelte, sweet and smart as a whip."

"Six-fifty!"

"I hear six-fifty for the honey with honey hair, do I hear six seventy-five, six seventy-five…"

Paige felt her legs weaken. Please God, make this end. "This is a mistake, George," she whispered to the auctioneer, her voice hoarse and low. "I'm not number—"

"Seven hundred!"

"That's more like it," George bellowed into the microphone. "I hear seven hundred, seven hundred, do I hear seven-fifty?"

He launched into the forced staccato that had enthralled the crowd all night, and someone yelled out a higher amount. The auctioneer's drone rose in intensity as he dared and defied them to up the ante.

"Eight-fifty!"

"Nine hundred!"

Her legs would never hold. George spun her again. Twirling, Paige caught a glimpse of Walker, still talking to the other man, but the light prevented her from seeing who it was.

"Nine-fifty!" The shout came from the back of the room.

That silenced the crowd for a moment, no doubt because they neared the thousand dollar figure that usually stopped the bidding.

Her cousin laughed at something his companion said, and leaned back, momentarily blocking the blinding light and giving Paige a straight shot at the man sitting next to Walker.

"One thousand dollars!"

She heard the amount called out from the back, but her gaze locked on wolflike gray eyes that devoured her. A spray of goose bumps cascaded down her spine as they stared at each other.

"Fifteen hundred!" The bid was shouted from the far left side of the crowded room, followed immediately by another.

But the lights seemed to fade, the shouting muted, and the merciless bidding drowned out. She simply couldn't tear her gaze from the handsome stranger who stared right back at her. Who was he? Who had Walker invited to this fund-raiser? Then he lifted his lips in a provocative half smile.

Whoever he was, he was a heartthrob.

"Two thousand!" With the blood rushing through her head, Paige barely heard the crazy bid barked from the far right side of the room.

The auctioneer roared with glee and urged the frenzy onward.

A trickle of perspiration snaked between her shoulder blades and she tried to swallow, still unable to look away from the man's riveting gaze.

Then he winked. So subtle, so sneaky, no one else could possibly have seen his secret message. But she did. And it sent an involuntary shudder through her body.

"Ten thousand dollars."

The auctioneer froze and looked toward the front table. "Did I hear…?"

He *couldn't.* He couldn't have said that. The wolf with gray eyes stood to an impressive height. Backlit by a spotlight and looking like a monarch making his pronouncement, his half smile widened to a predatory grin. "Ten thousand dollars for Paige Ashton."

For a long time the room remained soundless, then the gavel slammed so hard the podium vibrated and Paige's knees nearly buckled.

"Congratulations, sir, you've bought yourself one expensive evening out!"

His gaze never wavered from her. "Worth every penny."

"What the hell did you do that for?"

Matt Camberlane grinned at Walker Ashton's question. "I couldn't stand to see her suffer," he declared, his gaze skimming the stage for another glimpse of her. That had been true, but Matt knew that his life-long competitive streak had just seized him. No way that pretty woman was going out with any of the sharks in this room. At least not with any *other* shark in the room.

Walker burned Matt with a threatening stare. "She's my cousin. She wasn't up for bid. I told you, she's running the event."

"Precisely why I had to rescue her."

"She doesn't need your kind of rescuing."

Matt attempted a "Who me?" look that he knew didn't work on his friend. "I just told you, I've sworn off the opposite sex. You may have found the holy grail of love with Tamra, but I am not meant to drink from that ultimate cup of happiness." To underscore his point, he drained his goblet of Ashton pinot noir. As he tilted his head back, he caught a flash of butter-yellow silk behind the temporary stage and curtain. She'd get away for sure, if he didn't get back there and stake his claim.

He heard Walker snort. "Love? You weren't looking at her with love in your eyes, Matty boy. That was lust and I repeat—she's my *cousin*. We were raised together. Paige is like a little sister to me. Plus, she's been through hell the last couple of months."

"Chill, Walker. I'm not interested in her. I'm merely doing a little good deed. Some charity work." Still, he'd seen the intelligent glint in her almond-shaped eyes, and couldn't help noticing a few enticing curves on her slender body. He was most definitely interested. "She was seriously uncomfortable, couldn't you tell?" He stepped away from the table, determined to nab her. "It's for a good cause, remember?"

Before Walker could respond, the auctioneer started

yammering about number nineteen, and a skinny red-head slithered into the spotlights. Matt dashed between the round tables and made his way behind the velvet curtain.

He stood in the back for a moment, searching the darkened area for the woman who'd just caused havoc in his head…and a few other places, too.

"I don't know who you are, sir, but I guess I owe you ten thousand dollars."

Matt turned to find Paige behind him, barely reaching his chin, even in the strappy high heels he'd checked out while she'd been up on stage. They'd done very nice things for her legs. She stood with her shoulders locked in defiance, but her wide, sea-green eyes gave her a hint of vulnerability. She clasped a clipboard like a protective shield in front of her chest.

"Perhaps you don't understand how this works," he said, letting his gaze roam over her china-doll skin and settle on her slightly glossy, slightly parted lips. "I owe *you* ten thousand dollars. All you owe me is the pleasure of your company for an evening."

She shook her head. "No. You've made a mistake. A huge mistake. I'm not up—I'm not a bachelorette."

Disappointment squeezed his chest. "You're not?"

"I mean, I am technically, a…a—" she stammered, and then broke into a wide smile, holding out her hand. "I'm Paige Ashton. The assistant event coordinator."

He took the hand she offered and held it a second longer than he would a business associate. "I'm Matt Camberlane. The highest bidder."

"Matt *Camberlane?* The computer guy?"

He laughed. "I guess I've been called worse. Yeah, I'm the computer guy, and now I'm your next date, Miss Ashton. Where would you like to go for dinner?"

And breakfast, he thought with a flash of her writhing naked between the ridiculously expensive sheets of the five-star Napa resort he'd checked in to that afternoon.

"I am so sorry, Mr. Camberlane." He saw her take a deep breath and could have sworn she shuddered with it. "I can't."

"Can't?" He dipped his head closer to her and lowered his voice. "I don't know what that word means."

A slight flush darkened her cheeks. Damn, but she was pretty. Not an over-the-top vixen like most of the women who had been bobbing in the lights to get a better look at him. No, Paige Ashton was like hand-blown glass next to their plastic. Real and delicate and fragile.

"I'm sorry," she repeated. "You've bid on the wrong girl. I'm the wrong—"

"On the contrary." He placed a single finger on her lips to quiet her, a tiny bit of gloss sticking to him. "I don't see anything wrong with you at all."

She stepped back, out of his touch. "I'm afraid I—"

"Surely you wouldn't deny those poor families with sick children the benefits of all your hard work for this auction."

"I said I'll pay for your mistake."

He closed the space she'd made but didn't touch her again. Even though he really wanted to. "And I'm telling you, I *didn't* make a mistake."

"Ten thousand was way, way too much," she said.

He shrugged, a smile tugging at his lips. "Hey, it's a jungle out there. Survival of the biddest."

She started to laugh, but the voice of the auctioneer screeched from a loudspeaker beside them. "Sold to the gentleman at table eleven! And that brings our auction to a close."

"Are you just about finished here?" he asked, already imagining a moonlit stroll around the vineyard.

The speaker crackled with the next announcement, answering for her. "But the night isn't over. If you bidders would be kind enough to open your wallets for the cashiers, you can get to know your future dates with some dancing, courtesy of White Lightning."

The amplifier whined with a second of electronic feedback, then suddenly shut off, leaving them staring at each other in an unexpected silence.

"I have to work," she finally said. "But, please, let me fix this. Your donation was wonderfully generous and will go a long way to helping the families of children with cancer. One of the ladies didn't get a chance to go onstage. Number eighteen." She glanced at her papers and ran a finger over a list along the side. "Tiffany Valencia. Lovely girl." She looked up at him. "Gorgeous, in fact. I'll go arrange for you to meet her. You'll see—"

He took the clipboard from her hands and dropped it square on the wood floor with a resounding slap. "I don't want Tiffany Valencia," he said quietly. "I paid ten thousand dollars for Paige Ashton."

The color drained from her cheeks as she held his gaze. "Do you always get what you want, Mr. Camberlane?"

"Always." He added another wink to soften the next statement. "And I want you."

The words, and the sincere, sexy way he said them, sent a crackle of sparks to every nerve ending in Paige's body.

But something told her that this legendary self-made gazillionaire, whose image graced the San Francisco society columns with supermodels glued to his toned, athletic body, had better things to buy with his money.

He'd never be interested in plain-brain Paige, as she believed the rest of her family secretly thought of her.

She moved to retrieve her clipboard, but he was too fast. He scooped it up before she'd bent her decidedly wobbly knees.

"The music is starting," he said.

"It is?" She tore her attention from him to see the lead singer of White Lightning stepping up to the microphone. Good God, she's lost all focus on the event. "Yes, well, I have to—I have to—"

"You have to dance with me."

"I'm working," she insisted.

"No. You're dancing." He set the clipboard on a box next to the stage.

Jeez, the man was single-minded. Could he have wanted her that much? The impossible thought made her dizzy. Or maybe it was the sensation of his powerful hand on her lower back as he guided her around the stage to the dance floor set up in the middle of the room.

Wordlessly they joined the bachelorettes and their "dates" who'd already started swaying to the first ballad. As he pulled her into his chest, she realized with a start that his heart was pounding as steadily as hers. For some reason, that sent a new and wild exhilaration tumbling through her. He tightened his grip so her breasts pressed against the steely muscles of his chest. And that...oh, boy, *that* sent an even wilder exhilaration through her.

She didn't dare look up at him as he took her right hand and settled his comfortably around her waist. What did she even know about Matt Camberlane?

She knew that he'd started Symphonics, a successful company that specialized in music-oriented software. She knew he'd broken ground with the recording industry and solved some of the copyright problems that had plagued it, making millions for his efforts.

She knew he'd attended Berkeley with Walker a decade ago, but didn't realize they were still friends.

As they caught the rhythm of the song, she sneaked a peek over his substantial shoulder to where his dark-brown hair touched the collar of his shirt, a hint of golden chestnut at the tips. Her head brushed the hard angle of his jaw and she closed her eyes for a moment, remembering how his handsome face softened when he smiled.

She also knew that Matt Camberlane was flat-out magnificent. And that Paige Ashton was way out of her league.

Even in heels, he towered over her, fitting her comfortably in the nook of his neck and chest. She had to restrain herself from running her hands along the luxurious linen of his white shirt just to feel the male hardness beneath it.

With a sigh, she realized she should stop swooning and start talking. But small talk had never been her strong suit. She was an observer. And he offered plenty to observe.

"You should be very proud of yourself," he said into her ear.

Grateful for the chance to make conversation, she leaned back and looked up into his gun-metal-gray eyes. "I think the whole event has gone quite well, thank you."

"I mean for getting up on that stage and helping out."

She shook her head. "I can't take credit for any brilliant idea. I was just trying to tell the auctioneer that one of the girls was missing."

"Then it was my good luck." His smile was absolutely immoral.

In fact, everything about him indicated he was not a man to be toyed with. Nor was he the kind that would toy with her. She had never attracted powerful men; perhaps her father had scared them off, or perhaps her introverted personality had bored them.

She tried to lean back, but his hand held her securely against him, somehow managing to maintain blissful contact between their chests, their stomachs, their legs.

She recognized the last verse of the song. The dance was nearly done. Relief warred with disappointment.

"I really have to make sure the dessert table is still stocked. And I have to coordinate the cashiers and I have to—"

Still holding her hand, he reached under her chin and tipped her face toward him. "Are you scared of me, Paige?"

Petrified. "What a silly question. I just feel sorry that you spent—"

"Then why are you shaking?"

She stilled her step, hoping that would help the involuntary quiver that had started in her stomach the moment their bodies touched.

A million phony explanations swirled through her head: she was cold; she was worried about details; she was sorry he'd spent all that money on her.

She certainly wasn't going to admit that *he* made her shake. "Do you live in the Bay Area?"

As soon as she said it, she realized that sounded as though she cared where he lived. As though it mattered to her.

"I live in Half Moon Bay, near my office in San

Mateo. But I came up to Napa for the weekend. So, we can start our date right now and go straight through until Monday, if you like."

Heat washed over her at the thought. She liked. Oh, yes, she did.

"Or I'll settle for dinner tomorrow night," he said.

Why was he doing this? Men didn't flirt with Paige Ashton. She was too aloof, too quiet and usually too smart to play this kind of game. A game she'd undoubtedly lose. She closed her eyes and let her forehead rest on his shoulder with a soft sigh.

He nestled her closer. "Is that a yes?"

"No."

He chuckled in her ear. "Is that a maybe?"

"No."

He lowered his head and brought his lips so close to her cheek that she could feel the warmth of his breath. "Is that an 'I'll think about it and let you know, Matt'?"

The desire to turn toward his mouth, to close that centimeter of space and taste his lips nearly knocked her over.

"I'll think about it and let you know, Matt."

"I knew you'd come around."

He did? The only thing Matt Camberlane exuded more than sex appeal was raw confidence. And that, Paige realized as she inhaled the masculine, musky scent of him, was precisely what made her shake.

Paige Ashton had virtually disappeared from his side when their dance ended. He'd seen her gliding about the massive reception hall, quietly giving instructions, signaling waiters and assistants to change the lighting, adjust the sound system, bus the tables, refresh the glasses. She had effectively managed to stay out of the limelight, and much too far away from him.

He found ways to linger as the event wound down to a conclusion well after midnight. While he waited, he'd plunked down a check for ten grand made out to Candlelighters of Northern California, and had another glass of wine with Walker and his fiancée, Tamra, but neither made any mention of his cousin or the bid for a date with her. When the crowd thinned to almost nothing, the wait staff started yanking tablecloths and stacking chairs.

Still, he waited. Something told him she'd be back. As always, drawn to music, he shot the breeze with the lead singer as the band packed up. Matt purposely didn't mention his name—any musician would recognize it—but he did find out that the piano belonged to the Ashton Estate and that the band wouldn't be moving it.

The wait staff seemed preoccupied and unconcerned with what was happening on the stage, so he pulled out the bench and threaded his fingers, bending them back and giving them a shake. He hadn't played in a few weeks, but the sight of a grand piano usually stirred him. As did the sight of a fine-looking woman whom he wanted.

So, while he waited for her to appear again, he plunked out the first four measures of "Come Fly with Me." The bass player looked up from the mess of cables he was untangling, surprised.

"Like the old stuff, eh?"

Matt just grinned. Yep, he was Sinatra reborn. Only he couldn't sing a note. The words played in his head, on key and in Frankie's voice, while his fingers moved as if they had a mind of their own.

He closed his eyes and saw…yellow silk. Layers of soft, touchable, golden-brown hair. Almond-shaped green eyes…or were they blue? Depended on the light. And the uncertainty in them.

He smiled, thinking of how he'd steamrolled her. But the wisp of a woman had held her own against his will. She held herself pretty nicely against his body, too. The memory of her slender legs brushing against him, of her delicate breasts pressed against his chest forced him to reposition himself on the piano bench.

It had been a good long time since Matt had pursued a woman with any enthusiasm. Before his abomination of a marriage, they pretty much fell at his feet. After Brooke he'd been so cautious he'd avoided women for anything but mindless sex. But it had been two years since his quick and fairly clean divorce from the San Francisco social climber. His bank account had rebounded nicely, but his heart hadn't.

Not that Brooke Carlysle had broken his heart. No, she just left scars as deep as if she'd scraped it with acrylic nails, ensuring that he'd never again take that risk. He hadn't really loved her, he thought, as he transitioned effortlessly into an old Cole Porter tune. But he'd trusted Brooke. That was worse.

Plus, she'd represented something a kid from Modesto, with an alcoholic father and a trailer-jumping mother always wanted. Respect. Credibility. Acceptance.

He opened his eyes and let his gaze drift over the elegantly appointed hall. Flanked by French doors with heavy silk draperies and sparkling marble floors, the room could easily have been the formal ballroom at any palace in the world. And this was just another room in Paige Ashton's *home.*

His fingers paused momentarily on the keyboard as he finished with a flourish. His eyes still closed, he lifted his hands and let them drop on his thighs, a little disgusted that the music hadn't soothed him and old thoughts had plagued him.

Matt Camberlane was no longer the poor kid who managed to swing a degree from Berkeley thanks to the largesse of the U.S. Army and its ROTC program. He was no longer a struggling computer nerd who left the military with discipline and muscles but not a whole lot else. His fascination with technology, combined with a bone-deep love of music had translated into wealth beyond his childhood imaginings, and a lifetime of security and comfort. Anyone who didn't respect or accept him could screw themselves.

He played the opening of "I've Got You Under My Skin."

A sweet, clear voice sang the first line. With a start, he opened his eyes and saw…yellow.

For a moment they just looked at each other. He expected her to sing the next line, but she didn't and his fingers stilled. The air damn near popped between them.

"The workers are here to break down the stage," she finally said.

"Then that'll have to be my last number." He stood and gathered his jacket from where he'd flung it over the piano. "You have a very pretty voice."

She smiled but didn't say anything as she started back down the side stairs of the stage. He followed her until she slowed her step and he nearly bumped into her.

Turning, she shot him a serious look. "The party's over, Mr. Camberlane."

Actually, it hadn't started. "I need to know what time you want me to pick you up tomorrow."

Her eyes narrowed slightly. "I am so sorry for the misunderstanding. I hope you'll let me arrange for a refund of your donation."

It was the little hitch in her voice that got him. He held up a hand in surrender. "I wouldn't dream of taking a refund," he said. "It's a great cause and I'm happy to donate. And the apology is mine to offer."

He slipped into his jacket, noting the slackness of her jaw and the slight surprise in her expression at his sudden change of heart. Or was that disappointment?

"It was a great party," he added. "Every detail was—" The flash of insight was so brilliant, it should have blinded him. Why the hell didn't he think of it sooner? "In fact, I was so impressed, I'd like to reserve the estate for Halloween."

"Excuse me?"

"Are you booked?"

She shook her head slowly and frowned. "Not that I know of—but what's happening on Halloween?"

"Symphonics has picked the date to launch our new software product, the VoiceBox, that turns any computer into a karaoke machine. I just met with the product-development team last night and the last of the bugs has been worked out. We need a venue for about four hundred computer retailers, media and industry types and at least fifty of my employees for the VoiceBox launch party." He glanced around the room. "This place would be perfect."

"Halloween is less than four weeks away." She folded her arms and pursed her lips in doubt. "We usually plan events that large many, many months in advance."

"The computer industry moves at lightning speed. I have to get this product out and into stores for Christmas. And before any competitor gets wind of it."

"I don't know…"

"My Marketing department is excellent, but I would personally oversee the entire event." *And the event planner.* "We could meet, say, tomorrow night? At the French Laundry at seven."

The hint of a smile danced in those blue…no, no, they were definitely *green* eyes. "A business meeting at one of the finest restaurants in California?"

"Hey, that's my style. Bring a contract and ideas." He buttoned the single button on his jacket and grinned at her. "Strictly business."

Her defiant shoulders unlocked just enough to tell him he'd won. "Okay. My sister will be doubly pleased that we made the numbers tonight and I nailed a new account."

"Happy to accommodate your career aspirations. Should I pick you up here?"

She shook her head quickly. "Not for a meeting. I'll meet you at the restaurant."

Okay, a point to the lady for keeping it businesslike. "See you tomorrow, then."

He took one step backward, even though everything in him wanted to go in the other direction and plant a victory kiss on her appealing mouth. But that would definitely negate the "strictly business" promise he'd just made.

A promise he had no intention of keeping.

# Two

**M**att Camberlane either had to have been planning this dinner for months or his name carried so much weight that he managed to obtain what few mortals can: reservations at the French Laundry.

That thought was momentarily lost as Paige drove up Highway 29 toward the restaurant in Yountville, because she passed the rolling hills of Louret Vineyards. She glanced toward the entrance of the estate that her four half siblings called home. She hadn't seen any of them since she'd had lunch with Mercedes last month—one of her recent efforts to close the rift that only seemed to grow wider since their father's horrible murder last May.

Mercedes had been kind but preoccupied. And she hadn't been able to convince Paige that Mercedes's brother, Eli, would back off on his quest to have Spencer Ashton's will reversed.

As always Paige could see both sides of the Ashton

family's ever-complicated story. Her father had basically ensured this kind of turmoil by turning his back on his four children by Caroline Lattimer, and only acknowledging the family he'd created with Paige's mother. He'd done it in life, by ignoring Cole, Eli, Mercedes and Jillian, and he'd done it in death by leaving them out of his will. But Paige refused to believe her father was the god-awful man everyone made him out to be; as his youngest child, she was determined to see her father in a positive light.

Well, not really his *youngest* child, she corrected herself. Not since baby Jack had come into the picture, the surprise "love child" of Spencer and his last mistress. She made a mental note to make a visit to Louret next week, both to finally meet little Jack and try another pass at fence mending.

Just outside of town she turned onto Washington Street and saw the rustic two-story stone structure built as a French steam laundry in the late 1800s. But in that unassuming building, and in the lush gardens surrounding it, about sixty people a night were treated to the finest gourmet dinners served anywhere. And no one—well, practically no one—could get reservations without waiting at least two months.

Obviously Matt Camberlane wasn't "no one."

That wild, warm feeling she'd experienced last night spread through her again at the thought of him. She smoothed the skirt of the simple blue suit she'd chosen, as if that could wipe away the effect he had on her. On the passenger seat rested a leather binder containing an Ashton Estate Winery event contract, typed and ready for his signature. *Strictly business.*

But, oh, his attention had been far from professional last night. That man did things to her body and brain that they certainly didn't teach her in business school. Not that she took him seriously. Not for a minute. He must have some other reason for flirting with her.

She simply wasn't the kind of woman men played with. She was attractive enough, but Paige knew she lacked the vivaciousness and charm that appealed to most men. When she looked in the mirror, she saw serious hazel eyes that seemed a little too big for her small features, and plain brown hair that had none of the sassiness of the bottle blondes and redheads who'd paraded across that stage seeking a bid.

She shook her head at the thought of the bid that she got from Matt Camberlane. Men like Matt Camberlane—big, gorgeous, successful, self-assured, intriguing men—usually looked right through the Paige Ashtons of the world.

So what was that magic buzzing between them last night?

Pulling into the back parking lot, she found a spot next to a sleek silver sports car, grabbed the binder and a small handbag and climbed out.

Instantly her senses were assaulted by the rich smell of Napa's earth and the heady scents of fresh rosemary and mint. Herb gardens tumbled around the ancient building, a riot of lavender and green. A cool autumn breeze lifted her hair as she paused to drink in the beauty of the recently harvested hillsides, bathed in streaks of gold and ginger as the sun dipped into the western slopes.

Taking a deep breath for confidence, she rounded the restaurant to a tiny front patio darkened by a vine-covered overhang. There, her senses were assaulted again. By Matt.

And all her determination to treat this meeting as

strictly business melted into a pool of liquid heat that spread from her chest, through her tummy and straight down to the most feminine part of her.

He stood facing away from her, his attention focused on the glorious scenery. He wore an off-white shirt that stretched nicely across his broad back, tucked into elegant dark trousers. A sports jacket hung next to him, over the stone wall that enclosed the porch, his expression impassive. The setting sun cast a warm glow on his dark-brown hair that grazed his collar, adding a golden luster to the ends.

Paige's hands literally itched to touch that hair. To run her fingers through the length of it, then over the solid muscles of his shoulders, his chest. Down, down...

She swallowed against the erotic image that took hold of her brain.

Strictly business, Paige Ashton. She cleared her throat. "Pretty, isn't it?"

At her question, he turned and flashed that wicked smile as his gaze swept over her appreciatively. "It certainly is."

Oh, she'd walked right into that one.

He lifted his sports coat without taking his attention from her. "You have a habit of sneaking up on me." He slipped into the jacket, denying her a view of his broad shoulders but taking on a different, more sophisticated look.

"I'm quiet, in case you haven't noticed."

His gaze slid over her face again, dipping down to her throat and chest, making her wonder if she should have worn something buttoned higher instead of a V-neck shell. "I notice everything," he said softly. "For instance, I notice you came armed with a briefcase."

She shifted the thin portfolio from one hand to the other. "The contract," she told him. "I promised my sister Megan I'd nail down the Halloween event."

He guided her toward the entrance. "Walker tells me Megan is happily married and pregnant, and delighted to let you step into her shoes at the estate."

"She's happy and pregnant, yes," Paige agreed, "but hasn't exactly handed over the event-planning reins entirely to me. The auction was my first solo act."

"Really? I'd call it an astounding success."

She glanced up at him. "Thanks to one especially generous bidder."

He just winked at her, that secret, sexy wink that curled her toes. Then an older maître d' greeted Matt with a huge smile and an air of familiarity. "Good evening, Mr. Camberlane. Your table is ready." Somehow it sounded like it was just that—*his* table.

In a moment they were seated at an intimate table for two next to a window. "His" table was not exactly the strictly business setting she'd hoped for, leaving her to wonder just how often he dined here with women. One look at him answered that question. Often.

She tamped down the thought and listened to Matt exchange pleasantries with the maître d' about a new sommelier, a wine expert he'd brought over from France.

As soon as they were alone, he focused on her, the intensity of his silver-gray gaze nearly taking her breath away. "I would have introduced you," he said. "But I didn't want to put you in the awkward position of discussing the wine list."

She knew exactly what he was talking about. "They don't serve Ashton wine here."

Ashton wine was good—great in some years, especially under her older brother Trace's fine management—but the exclusive restaurant leaned more toward the impossibly expensive and elite wines. Like Louret.

"It wouldn't make me uncomfortable to discuss their cellar," she assured him. "No doubt it will come up when the new sommelier makes his recommendations." She gave him a direct, serious look. "Regardless of the less-than-stellar media coverage my family has received, I remain proud of the name."

He nodded in agreement. "As you should be. You can't take the blame for the troubles your father inflicted on the family."

"My father's *murder* inflicted the trouble," she corrected. "My half brothers and sisters have simply fanned the fire and made things worse. Although," she lifted one shoulder in a shrug, "I understand their position."

"That's sisterly of you."

"Family is…" Taking her napkin and smoothing it on her lap, she met his gaze again, purposely not finishing the thought. "How much has Walker told you?"

"Walker has always been very candid about your family. He told me when we first met as roommates in Berkeley the whole story of how his uncle Spencer arranged to take him and Charlotte and raise them as your siblings."

"And no doubt he told you that my father told Walker his mother was dead, and not living on a Sioux reservation."

"Yes," Matt nodded. "Like I said, he's never hidden anything from me. But—" he gave a rueful smile "—he's been a little preoccupied since Tamra came into the picture and they began establishing the Sioux scholarship program. So what I know of the recent drama I've read in the papers or heard, if you'll forgive the awful pun, through the grapevine."

She laughed softly. "Grapevines are for wine, not gossip."

The waiter, who also seemed to know Matt well, stopped by to light the candle and exchange pleasantries but didn't even discuss the menu. Dinner at the Laundry was a lengthy, multicoursed affair dictated by the whims and moods of the world-famous chef.

A long, intimate affair. By candlelight. With wine.

Paige automatically reached for her leather binder when the waiter left. "I haven't drawn up a specific theme for your event, yet—"

In one smooth move, he flipped the portfolio closed, making the candle flicker with the puff of air from the sudden movement. "That can wait."

Paige gave him a sharp look. "We have business to discuss."

"I'm sorry. You're absolutely right." He reached into the breast pocket of his jacket and produced a silver pen. "Give it to me to sign and then we'll be done."

She hesitated and leaned back, the folder against her chest. "You're too savvy a businessman to sign just anything without reading it first."

"All that contract should say is that Symphonics, Inc. has reserved the reception hall of Ashton Estate for an event on October 31."

Paige had to admit it really didn't contain too much more detail. "There's a lot of fine print," she said, knowing by the look in his eyes that didn't matter. Once they were done discussing business, this dinner went back to *date* status. For some reason that thought sent a tremor of trepidation straight through her.

She could handle Matt Camberlane on a business level—after all, she'd graduated from business school with honors, the youngest in her class. But as a date?

He reached over and gently wrested the portfolio from her hand. "We'll go over the fine print and details next week," he announced. "We can meet in my office on Monday."

He opened the portfolio, shuffled through the pages and scribbled his name on the last one. With a satisfied smile, he handed the whole package back to her. "Now you can relax."

Yeah, right. "I am relaxed." She set the folder against the leg of her chair with an air of resignation. Well, he *paid* for a date.

He leaned forward, as though he'd like to eliminate the space and table between them. "I would imagine everyone in your family has strong opinions and volatile emotions where your father's will and death are concerned. I'm intrigued by your levelheaded view of the situation."

His demeanor said he was intrigued by more than that, but she played along and answered the question. "I believe there are two sides to every story. My half brothers and sisters are understandably crushed that my father had..." She tried to think of a less vicious word than *abandoned* to describe what her father had done to the four children he had with Caroline Lattimer, but couldn't. There was no word other for it. "They—especially the oldest, Eli—are simply determined to get what they think is rightfully theirs." And since the estate had been in the Lattimer family long before Spencer had renamed it Ashton and kept it in his divorce from Caroline, Paige couldn't help but understand Eli's position.

"Any progress on the murder investigation? The media seems to be reporting nothing."

Paige closed her eyes for a moment, then blew out a

slow breath as the image of her father, shot point-blank in his own office, darkened her mind. "Not really. At the moment, the police are honing in on some blackmail threats my father had received and a numbered bank account that he'd mysteriously kept well stocked."

His eyes softened a bit at the crack in her voice. "I got the impression that most of the Ashtons were…" he paused and tilted his head as he obviously searched for his own euphemism. "Not that distraught over your father's death."

*Most* of them weren't, she silently agreed. "He was my father," she said simply. "Everyone deserves to be mourned."

The sommelier approached their table, and the conversation turned to wine, and once again Matt Camberlane impressed her. Not only had he gracefully handled the issue of her last name, he knew an awful lot about wines.

"Not bad, for a computer guy," she said with a smile once they were alone.

He laughed. "I can thank Walker. A wine expert is a good roommate to have in college. We never got drunk on anything but the good stuff."

She seized on the chance to turn the conversation toward him. "Did you go to business school at Berkeley, as well?"

"I didn't go to graduate school," he said evenly. "I went into the Army."

It was her turn to be surprised. "You did?"

"Didn't Walker ever tell you? I was at Berkeley on an Army ROTC scholarship. I had to do my time for Uncle Sam to pay for the privilege." She heard a note of defensiveness creep into his voice, making her heart clutch a bit.

"Walker's only bragged that the boy wonder of Symphonics was his old college buddy. Did you like the Army?"

"I liked the discipline, the order of it. I got the opportunity to work on some amazing electronics, really cutting edge stuff. It all led me to where I am today, so I don't complain." He gave her a seductive smile. "By the way, I'm a wonder, but no boy."

"You're a flirt," she responded, trying to ignore the tightening low in her tummy at his words and tone. "And I'm not."

He slid a water glass to the left and closed his hand over hers, never taking his gaze off her. "That's what I like about you, Paige Ashton."

It was easy to believe him and very hard to ignore her body's response.

Several hours passed as they sampled nouvelle servings of foie gras, red pepper crostini and sautéed moulard, complimented by a bottle of extraordinary Louret wine. By the time they'd finished sharing a champagne gellée dessert, Matt knew one thing for sure about Paige Ashton—besides the fact that she wasn't a flirt:

He wanted her.

He liked her quiet spirit, her keen intelligence and the way her lower lip sort of trembled when he captured, and purposely held, her gaze. He liked her elegant table manners, her smooth ability to keep a conversation going, her enticing little cleavage when she leaned forward.

Yep. He wanted her.

"Let's go for a ride," he suggested as they stepped into the moon-washed patio, nearly the last of the customers to leave.

She flattened the portfolio against her chest again like thin leather armor. "Thank you, but I really have to get back to the estate."

"It's Saturday night, Paige." He took her arm possessively and slid it into his elbow. "The stars are out, the moon is—" he squinted into the sky "—half-full and I have less than three thousand miles on a brand new sports car. You could be the first girl to ride in it."

"But not the last," she said quickly.

He feigned a wounded look. "You think I'm a cad."

"A cad? Do people use that word anymore?"

He laughed as they reached his car. "You tell me. You're a smart girl."

"Smart enough to say thank you for the lovely dinner and your business. What time is our meeting on Monday?"

He considered how simple it would be to turn her in his arms, ease her against the side door of his Ferrari and pull her delicious little body into his.

The thought had its effect on him, so he did precisely the opposite and stepped away from her. No making out in a parking lot for this lady. Seducing Paige would take longer, and the place had to be perfect.

"I'll clear my schedule for you on Monday," he offered politely. "What time can you be in San Mateo?"

"Ten o'clock."

"Ten it is. We'll go up to San Francisco and have lunch afterward."

She laughed softly. "How can you think of lunch after all that fantastic food?"

"You make me hungry," he admitted with a teasing smile.

Her eyes darkened just enough to communicate that she got his meaning. "Matt…" She stepped back. "I don't mix business and pleasure."

"Then tear up that contract," he joked.

She smiled and clutched the binder. "Not a chance. We're going to have fun with this event. Everyone in costumes, fantastic music—"

"Costumes?" He choked a little. "I hadn't thought of costumes."

"It's Halloween," she countered. "Of course there'll be costumes. I need to know all the details of the new product—the VoiceBox, is it? I'll need to start thinking of a theme for the event."

"Music. That's the only theme I'm interested in."

"Perfect. Come as your favorite musician. Who's yours?"

"Sinatra." He didn't even hesitate. "I'm his number-one fan."

That won him the sweetest smile. "Then you'll come as Old Blue Eyes himself."

He laughed at the thought. "Just don't make me sing."

"But you could play. I heard you last night. You're very good."

"Hardly. But I like the idea of musician costumes. The product is a computer karaoke, so we could have a lot of fun with that."

"Great. I'll work on it for Monday morning."

He suddenly hated the idea of Sunday stretching out before him without her. "I'm staying at Auberge du Soleil, in Napa," he said. "Let's get together tomorrow and work on it then."

Her eyes narrowed just enough to let him know she was thinking about it. "Another business meeting?"

"Call it whatever you want, Paige." He couldn't resist sliding his hands up her arms, over her narrow shoulders, letting her hair tickle his skin. He held her delicate face between his hands, his focus dropping to that lower lip he wanted so much to taste. "I happen to think business and pleasure is a great mix."

One kiss. That was all he wanted. One quick, warm, good-night kiss.

As he leaned toward her, he felt her tense up, but as soon as their lips touched, she relaxed. He tilted his head slightly, tasting a whisper of sweet sorbet that clung to her lips.

No. One kiss was not going to be enough.

But it was all he would take now. "Tomorrow?" he asked, keeping his mouth just a breath from hers. "We'll have a picnic in the olive grove at Auberge."

Her little sigh of resignation warmed his lips and he fought back a grin. There was nothing Matt loved more than winning. "One stipulation, however," he added.

She gave him a questioning look.

"Leave that binder at home. This won't be work, I promise."


As Paige tiptoed down the main stairs of the estate the next morning, she heard a few familiar family voices in the dining room, and caught a whiff of Irena Hunter's incomparable eggs Benedict floating from the cavernous kitchen.

She slipped past the butler's pantry and eyed the pot of fresh-brewed coffee tucked into the corner. After last night's meal, coffee was all she wanted. And after a sleepless night of reliving one breathless kiss and imagining many more, she needed the caffeine.

"I didn't hear you come in last night, honey."

Paige winced at the sound of her mother's voice coming from the dining room. She almost asked, "Since when did you listen for me?" but swallowed the retort.

Lilah Ashton may not have been the model for mother-hood, but in her own way she cared about her children.

Filling her cup, Paige simply called out a morning greeting.

"What time did you get in?" Walker's question was pointed and direct, the way he always was.

Taking a deep breath and a sip of strong, black cof-fee, she made her way through the hallway into the din-ing area. As always the table was set with fine china, crystal and snow-white linens. For just a minute Paige longed to curl up at a cozy kitchen table, drink coffee from a chipped mug and skim the Sunday paper like nor-mal people.

But they weren't normal. They were Ashtons.

The thought made her smile, as she took her usual seat.

"What are you smiling about?" Tamra looked re-markably relaxed for a woman who, just three months earlier, had been rather overwhelmed by all that was Ashton when Walker had brought her home from the reservation. He'd gone to find his long-lost mother and had unexpectedly found the love of his life, as well.

Paige widened her smile for Tamra, happy that she and Walker, having built their own world away from the estate, had decided to stay for the whole weekend after the fund-raiser.

Tamra's deep-chocolate gaze shifted pointedly to her fiancé, then back to Paige. "What are you smiling about?" she repeated. "You didn't answer my ques-tion."

"Or mine," Walker added.

Family. They certainly made her life…interesting. "We contracted a Halloween event to launch Sym-phonics' new karaoke computer product, the Voice-

Box," she said. "Maybe you two will come back up here for it. A costume party—come as your favorite musician."

Lilah reacted with a delighted coo. "How creative! Let's see…" Her blue eyes twinkled as she looked fondly at Tamra. "You could be Cher."

For a moment, Tamra's cheeks darkened, then she grinned. "She's a Cherokee, Lilah. I could never pull off Cher."

"Plus she must be near sixty by now," Walker added and held up his cup as Irena entered the room with a pot of coffee.

"I hope you're not talking about me, Mr. Walker." The housekeeper spoke quietly, but the comment elicited smiles all around.

"Not a chance," Walker reassured her with a teasing wink. "You're nowhere *near* sixty, Irena."

"As a matter of fact I am, Mr. Walker," she said as she poured coffee into his cup. "But you're sweet to say that."

Her warm smile was directed to Walker, but a sudden good feeling filled Paige as she watched the exchange. They had their quirks and problems, but this was her family. Extended and otherwise. And so, she remembered, were the virtual strangers at Louret Vineyards. Regardless of their father's deceptions and dalliances.

Once again she vowed to visit her half siblings in the next few days, but before she could take another sip of coffee, she felt Walker's intense dark stare return to her. When he wanted to know something, there was very little escaping.

"So," he said. "I take it your client contact will be the CEO himself."

She simply nodded and focused on the rim of her coffee cup.

"Be careful, little cousin," he said. "You can get burned when you play with fire."

Her head shot up. "I'm not playing with anything."

Lilah smoothed a strand of Merlot-colored hair and attempted a concerned frown. The Botox made forehead creases a thing of the past for her. "What are you talking about, Walker? What is she playing with?"

Paige felt the blood rise to her cheeks. "Nothing, Mother." She shot Walker a warning look. "Walker is imagining things."

He said nothing, but pinned her with that impassive stare, his half-Sioux blood evident in the sheer power of his look. Tamra put a gentle hand on his arm. "We really have to be going if we want to be back in San Francisco before noon," she said softly.

Walker nodded, his expression automatically softening at Tamra's touch.

Paige thanked Tamra for the reprieve with a quick look of appreciation. But part of her desperately wanted to know why Walker thought she was playing with fire. She'd ask him…sometime.

In the meantime that "fire" had warmed and attracted her. More than anything—or anyone—she'd ever met. She kept remembering the gentle kiss and how she wanted to open her mouth and take him in. The way her whole body just tingled when he looked into her eyes. The sound of his voice, so deep and low it vibrated her every cell when he said her name. The way he made her laugh and all their verbal volleying. His strong, clever, musician's hands. What they could do to her…

"Don't you think, Paige?"

She looked up at her mother's question and took a cue from her smiling face. Whatever they'd been discussing, it sounded like something she should agree to. She nodded and sipped, blessedly saved by Megan's familiar voice in the hall, followed by the sound of their brother Trace coming down the main steps and greeting her.

In a moment the Ashton dining room was filled with more family, and Paige quietly watched the interplay between them all. Megan's green eyes sparkled as she rubbed the rounded swell of her tummy. Walker and Tamra settled in to stay a few minutes longer and, without anyone seeming to intentionally steer the conversation, the talk automatically turned to Spencer Ashton's will and the investigation of his murder.

"Stephen is confident the discovery of these letters will be a major turning point in the case," Lilah said, referring to the family attorney who'd spent so much time at the estate lately. "He's meeting with investigators every day and keeping me informed every step of the way."

Paige's brother Trace leaned against the wall, stoic and strong as always, and deeply unhappy about the situation. He ran a hand over his jaw and blew out a frustrated breath. "There've been a lot of dead ends."

"There could be DNA on those letters, regardless of the fact that some are nearly ten years old." Megan's husband, Simon, held out a chair for Megan and casually brushed her long blond hair as he offered his opinion. "We need to give them time to run every possible test."

"It's taking too long," Lilah said with such disdain Paige could imagine her making a tsking sound. "I'm going to ask Stephen to pressure the investigators for more attention on the case."

"We need closure," Trace agreed, his green eyes—so like Megan's—narrowing. "Both families do."

Paige listened, as always, hearing and weighing each opinion. As the youngest and the quietest, her voice was rarely heard, but when she spoke, her siblings and cousin gave her their attention.

"I'm going to Louret on Tuesday," she announced, surprising herself with her definitive air. "I want to talk to Mercedes again." And meet my little brother, she added in her head. She didn't mention her father's illegitimate child in front of her mother.

Her comment sparked a flurry of discussion, but Paige just stood and took her coffee cup back into the butler's pantry.

Her mind wasn't on family issues today, she told herself as the heated voices droned on. Her mind—and her body—were elsewhere.

Maybe Matt was sincere in his attraction, she thought for the fiftieth time that morning. She'd find out today. And if she trusted him, if she believed him, she was more than ready to—

"Why are you grinning?" Megan had come up behind her in the hallway and slid a sisterly hug around Paige's waist. "These discussions usually get you teary-eyed or passionate about fairness, sweetie. I demand to know what—or *who*—put a smile on your face."

Paige turned and gazed at her sister. Pregnancy had only made her prettier, but obviously it hadn't dampened her controlling nature. "You *demand* to know?" Paige laughed lightly. "My mood seems to be of interest to everyone this morning."

Megan leaned against the granite counter of the butler's pantry and eyed Paige. "How did the *meeting* go last night?"

The emphasis was not lost on Paige. "Fine. We got the event."

"You look a little—" Megan's finger skimmed lightly under one of Paige's eyes "—tired."

Paige pulled back. "I'm doing the work of two people, remember? By the way, how's the morning sickness?"

"Getting better," Megan admitted, rubbing her tummy again. "I can keep down broth and crackers. Don't change the subject."

"I'm not." Part of her wanted to confide in Megan, to tell her the insane feelings that Matt Camberlane had evoked. But she held back. The rest of her family was twenty feet away, and she just wasn't ready to share anything. Maybe after this afternoon.

"Simon and I are going to drive up to Calistoga this afternoon and look for baby furniture in the antique stores," Megan said. "Come with us."

Paige shook her head. "No, thanks. I'm busy."

"Doing what?"

"Work," Paige replied, purposely vague.

"On a Sunday?"

"I'm meeting with the new client." Paige turned to pour a cup of coffee she no longer wanted. "We're having lunch at Auberge."

Megan lifted a lock of Paige's hair, as though she could whisper better into her sister's ear. "Sounds serious."

Paige laughed a little. "Misery loves company, huh?"

"Oooh." Megan giggled. "Misery, huh? This *is* serious. You know, I've seen Matt Camberlane."

Paige turned to read the expression that went with Megan's obvious implication.

"What?" Paige demanded. "What is that look for?"

Megan lifted a wary eyebrow and crossed her arms. "I've seen him, that's all."

"And…?"

"He's hot."

"And I'm not."

Megan shook her head. "You underestimate yourself, sweetie. You may be smart and have a string of degrees, but you're young. And inexperienced. Be careful."

She wasn't that inexperienced, Paige thought with a flashing memory of her one lover in college. What a disaster. Still, her family's warnings all pointed to the same truth: they didn't think that she could attract a man like Matt, that he was just toying with her, that she was out of her league.

Well, maybe they were wrong.

Instead of confiding her thoughts, Paige just tapped the slightly swollen belly between them with a teasing smile. "Yeah. Look what happened when you got too friendly with an event client."

They both laughed, remembering how Megan had provided the ultimate in event-planning service—pretending to be the bride. But her "marriage" ended up both real and happy.

"What's so funny back here?" Walker's booming voice broke their moment.

"Nothing, Walker," Megan assured him. "Paige and I were just discussing client relations."

Walker's eyes flashed for a moment, but Paige managed to slip out of the butler's pantry before he could say anything.

She'd been warned enough. She knew all about getting burned by fire. She also knew that fire provided heat and pleasure. And right now, she craved a little of both.

# Three

"**I**'ve never seen anyone nibble an olive with so much precision," Matt observed, watching the black calamata disappear in tiny increments into Paige's delicate mouth. Lucky little thing.

"I don't like to bite the pit," she told him, leaning back comfortably on the blanket they'd laid out when they began their leisurely picnic more than an hour earlier. "I'm a very careful person."

"Deliberate," he corrected, noticing the way the sun dappled through the thick olive tree branches, highlighting the lovely angles of her face. He never knew what "dewy" skin was until he saw hers in the sunlight. Creamy, pure, flawless. "If you were careful, you wouldn't be here. You're just deliberate."

She teethed around the pit some more and locked her gaze on him. Her ever-changing eyes had taken on an emerald hue in the shadows of the olive grove tucked away on a hillside beneath Auberge du Soleil. It matched the dark-green sweater she wore.

"I'm not sure I like the sound of that," she said with a slightly uncomfortable laugh. "What do you mean, if I were careful, I wouldn't be here? Are you dangerous?"

"I could be." He grinned and inched closer to her, liking the way their lounging positions lined up their bodies. Really liking the way her jeans fit over her narrow hips and slender legs.

He'd picked a very secluded area of the grounds, but knew that hotel guests could still invade their private spot at any moment. So he forced himself to focus on her face and not her sweet little body. But that was just as appealing, he realized.

"*Walker* thinks you're dangerous," she told him. "But I think you're..."

He looked at her expectantly, loving the way her gaze drank him up. "Yeah?"

"Cute. You're cute, I'll give you that."

He laughed. "Great. A cute computer guy. Don't you have anything nice to say about me?"

"You're smart."

"So are you."

She shrugged off that compliment. "Tell that to my family. Early college graduation, business school—none of it matters. I'm still the baby."

He leaned on his elbows and studied her. "Maybe you should strike out on your own. Leave the family business and show them what you're capable of when you're not under their watchful eyes."

"I plan on it." She plucked another olive from the container the concierge had packed for him. "But not until all of this unpleasant family business is resolved.

Megan needs my help, and I have an important job to do with my family."

"Which is?"

"I keep the peace." Her straight white teeth closed over the olive, jolting a sudden arousal in him. "I love these," she said with her eyes half-closed. "Better than grapes, in my opinion."

He laughed, moving a little closer. "That kind of talk could cause war in the wine-making family you are so determined to keep at peace."

She smiled and worked on the olive, further torturing him when she sucked a little juice from it. She was so much more relaxed than last night, he thought. As though she'd stopped fighting his attention and decided to enjoy it. And he was just the opposite—not relaxed at all.

The evening with her had left him hard and achy, sweating in the middle of the night and waking up with images of big green eyes. Or were they blue? Either way, his desire hadn't diminished since their evening together.

He couldn't pinpoint the precise characteristic of Paige that got to him. There were so many. He found her subtly beautiful, disarmingly intelligent and just hesitant enough to make him want to ease her against the blanket, wrap his legs around her and let her feel what she did to him.

He glanced around the rambling grounds of Auberge, the tips of the French-style rooftop visible over the lush greenery.

His suite was just a two-minute walk from where they were. Could he get her there? Could he seduce this delectable lady and give her the same pleasure he craved?

Of course he could. Seduction was never difficult for him. And he hadn't wanted a woman like this in so long. Since his divorce from Brooke he'd just gone through the motions, taking the ones who threw themselves at him. Lately not even those women interested him.

He forced his thoughts back to the conversation. "So, what would you do if you didn't work for Ashton Wineries?" he asked, breaking a piece of crusty bread and holding it out to her.

She shook her head, not quite finished with the calamata. "I'd like to run my own business."

He took a bite of the bread and brushed away the snowfall of flaky crumbs that fluttered on the blanket. "What kind?"

"Oh, I don't know. I'm very good with numbers and accounting," she looked at him and grinned. "How dull is that?"

"Nothing about you is dull, Paige." The comment won him a sweet flush on her cheeks and a glint of disbelief in her eyes.

"What's really important to me," she continued, dropping her gaze back to the basket between them, "is that I'm on my own. Without the guidance of big brothers and big sisters and big cousins."

He laughed softly. "Walker is one big cousin to deal with."

"He means well," she said defensively. "He feels he owes my father a huge debt of gratitude for taking him and his sister, Charlotte, into our home and raising them as a seamless part of our family."

"And that means he watches over you." Like a hawk, no doubt. A sliver of guilt wrapped around his gut for a moment. Maybe he shouldn't seduce her. Maybe he should…wait.

His body rebelled at the thought.

"I expect and appreciate his watchfulness, don't get me wrong." She wiped her hand on a linen napkin and dabbed the corners of her mouth. "And Megan's, and Trace's. And I love the family business, but it would be nice to do something away from the Ashtons. To be my own woman."

"And a fine woman she is," he said slowly, moving the basket that separated them.

Her eyes flashed in warning. "You're flirting again."

"Can't resist," he admitted. "You bring out the flirt in me."

She shook her head slowly. "I don't bring out the flirt in anyone."

"Where do you get this misinformed opinion of yourself?" he asked, surprised by her statement. "Don't you have any idea how attractive you are?"

"I'm not ugly," she agreed, but not wholeheartedly. "I'm just not one of those uninhibited, brash, bouncy women who enter duels of witty banter with men."

"I like that," he admitted, reaching over to touch the smooth skin of her hand. "I like you." Her eyes looked doubtful again. "You don't believe me."

"I want to believe you. I'm just a little…intimidated by you." She gestured around the secluded grove. "By this."

"An Ashton? Intimidated?" He threaded his fingers through hers. "I don't buy it for a minute."

She eased herself closer to him. Yes, this was going to be easy. And fun. He leaned toward her, close enough to feel the electrical charges singing in the air between them.

Unwinding his fingers from hers, he trailed a path up her arm, toward the soft flesh of her neck and throat.

When he lightly touched the skin just under her ear, her eyelids fluttered. He grazed along the edge of her delicate jaw, then traced the outline of her lips.

He felt her breath catch.

"You like that," he whispered.

She almost nodded, opening her eyes enough to capture his gaze. "I like you." The echo of his own admission was difficult for her, he could tell.

"You're such a flirt, Paige Ashton."

She started to laugh at that, but he leaned over and covered her mouth with his. As their lips met, her laugh stuttered into a moan that caught in her throat. As she opened to him, he tasted the delicious, tangy flavor of Greek olives on her tongue.

He tunneled his hand into her hair, holding her head with a strong, confident grip. She kissed him back, meeting his mouth with matching passion.

Easing her on to her back, he moved over her, so that they finally touched. Against the concave of her stomach, his arousal was impossible to hide. She sucked in a quick breath, her kiss halted momentarily.

"Just so you know," he whispered against her mouth. "I like you more."

She responded by resuming the kiss and lifting herself toward him, a move that sent every drop of blood in his body rushing to one place. He wanted her. His body hurt with swollen desire as he stroked her back, aching to glide his hand around and touch the delicate rise of her breast, itching to grasp her round rear end and bury himself between her legs.

Drawing a deep breath, he forced himself to do none of those things. "I think we're done here," he said softly.

She lifted her chin and gave him a stunned, hurt look. "We are?"

"Here," he explained. "In the olive grove. Let's go up to my suite."

Her eyes widened, and she tucked the corner of her lip between her teeth as the decision colored her expression. He swallowed every word of persuasion he knew. This was her choice.

"Okay."

Even to Paige, her simple word sounded raspy, aroused. As it should. She felt raspy and aroused. Her whole being sparked in anticipation, longing for more hot kisses, dying for his hands to engulf her entire body.

"Okay," he repeated, sounding a teensy bit surprised and a lot delighted. Didn't he think she wanted to go to his room?

Did he want her to say no?

She crushed the thought, hating her insecurities when everything about him had demonstrated just the opposite.

This wasn't a tough decision. Matt Camberlane was sexy, gorgeous, smart, and he wanted her. Her gaze dropped to the very obvious tent in his khaki pants, the sight of it both flattering and intoxicating.

As he folded up the blanket in one quick move and scooped up the remnants of their picnic, she made a feeble attempt to help, but he was much faster.

"I got it, sweetheart," he said, reaching for her hand to help her up. "Let's go."

Nice to know they were both in a hurry. That this electrifying, crazy, lusty attraction was mutual. The thought sent a little shiver through her, and he pulled her under his arm, holding the blanket and basket easily in his other hand. Instantly she felt safe. Safe and warm and protected by the power that was Matt.

In silence they climbed the stone stairs out of the grove. She barely glanced at the panorama of Rutherford Hills' rolling vineyards around them, didn't even notice the sun- and earth-toned cottages that made up the outer buildings of the luxury hotel and spa.

Together, they slipped into a side door, dropped the basket and blanket with the concierge, and headed up a set of back stairs. He must be staying in one of the luxurious upper suites, she thought. She'd been in one when friends from Los Angeles had stayed at the famous inn. The suites were huge. Would they even make it through the spacious living room to the bedroom?

Her heart rattled her whole chest, as he slid the key in the door, his own hands steady. Before he opened it, he froze for a moment, then tipped her face up to him with his other hand.

"You still have plenty of time to change your mind, Paige," he said softly. "I don't want you to feel…seduced."

She blew out a breath and smiled. "You're the one who should feel seduced, Matt."

His expression softened with a sexy half grin as he pushed the door open. "I love it when you flirt with me."

They'd never make it to the bedroom. At least, not dressed. As the door closed behind them, he didn't give her a second to even scan the glorious decor of the room. He pushed her right up against the door and pinned her there with his whole, heavenly, strong body.

His kiss was demanding and complete, his erection pressing into her stomach, making her want to hoist herself higher to get the hard ridge exactly where she wanted and needed it.

He reached under her sweater, the heat of his hand searing the skin of her waist. He murmured her name as their teeth tapped and their legs entwined. His hand moved higher and he sucked in a ragged breath as he covered the thin material of her bra and cupped her breast.

"You are so sexy, Paige," he whispered to her.

The words were the sweetest elixir, like the first-pressed wine. She moaned in response, leaning into him, giving him free access to stoke the fires in her body.

His thumb grazed her hardened nipple, swelling it like magic, sending waves of heat from her breasts down to her dampened crotch. All thoughts of decorum, all notions of propriety dissolved in her as his mouth trailed down her throat and their hips began to rock in a natural, marvelous rhythm.

Her hands flattened against his chest, finally able to touch him, hungry to get her fill of his substantial, solid body.

In one quick move he guided her to an oversize chaise longue near an unlit fireplace and lifted her sweater over her head, dropping it on the ground. Easing her back, he opened the front clasp of her bra and pushed it away, over her shoulders, then let it fall to the floor.

For a moment he just looked at her bare breasts, admiration and want turning his eyes slate-gray as he levered himself above her. His lips were parted, releasing tight, quick breaths.

Wordlessly he dropped his head and suckled one breast, the response flashing like a bolt of heat lightning in her body. Shuddering, she burrowed her fingers into his thick hair, as he teased her nipple with his tongue and then took more of her in his mouth.

She moved on instinct, driven by some basic, primal need she barely recognized. When he lifted his head, her hands roamed his chest, yanking at the buttons of his oxford shirt, aching to feel his flesh against hers.

With a gentle chuckle, he helped her remove his shirt, then returned to the delivery of wet, hungry kisses to her face and body. Their rhythm intensified as she rose to meet his hips and slide against his swollen manhood.

Time and space and sanity vanished from her senses, leaving her mind blank and her body in complete control. Deep in the core of her, a knot of desire and want tightened, pulling at her, twisting her low on the inside.

The need to have him inside her nearly made her cry out.

Reaching down, she slid open his belt buckle, tugged at the snap of his pants and grasped the heated skin of his shaft.

He moaned in appreciation of her touch, his eyes squeezed shut as though he simply couldn't take the pleasure. Her fingers almost encircled him, sliding up the length of him to caress the moistened tip.

Desire coiled through her as she imagined how he would feel inside of her. She had no doubt—*none*—that she wanted exactly that. In the darkest recess of her mind, she was aware that a lump had formed in her throat, an emotional juggernaut that was rivaled only by the throbbing ache between her legs. An unfamiliar twirling, swirling sensation of need spun through her, dizzying her.

He kissed her mouth again, as his talented fingers played with her nipples, his incredible body smothering hers.

He felt so *good*. So good she wanted to scream, but that tender pain in her throat grew tighter, and she choked out a desperate breath. But it sounded more like a sob.

Could this be happening? Could she have this kind of

power over Matt? Gorgeous, brilliant Matt? She hardly knew him, but she never wanted anything so completely.

Suddenly he stopped moving, his gaze locked on her face.

"What's the matter?" he asked, his voice strained and rough.

She shook her head. No, don't stop. Don't talk. Don't— Nothing," she managed.

"You're crying." It sounded more like an accusation than an observation.

Slowly she lifted a hand to her face. Her cheeks were wet—soaked, in fact. And the salty taste trickling in her mouth wasn't sweat.

She *was* crying.

She tried a quick laugh, but it came out as another sob. She wanted to curse herself, her childish, insecure self. Why was she crying?

"You have quite an effect on me," she finally said. "I don't know why I'm crying."

A dark expression colored his face. Gingerly he lifted his hands from her, placing them on the chaise and hoisting himself up.

"I do," he said simply.

The finality of his tone neutralized all the sensations zinging through her nerve endings. She reached for his arm, but he backed farther away. "C'mere, Matt."

She sounded desperate. Who cared? She was desperate. For more of his body, his mouth, his—

"No. We have to stop."

"What?" She pushed herself up on two hands, her jaw opened in shock. "Why?"

"We have to." In one move he was off her, refastening his pants, refusing her eye contact. Which hurt almost as much as his denial of *body* contact.

What was going on? "Matt? What are you doing?"

He wet his lips and ran his hand through his hair with a hand that now trembled nearly as much as her whole body, but still he didn't look at her.

With a deep sigh, he finally perched on the side of the chaise. He lifted her sweater from the ground, turned it right side out and gently laid it on top of her, covering her bare breasts.

All that erotic desire that had delighted her thudded to the bottom of her stomach. Of course. He didn't want her. She wasn't attractive. When you got right down to bare skin, she wasn't enough woman for him.

"I'm really sorry, Paige. I got carried away."

She just stared at him. "I think the carrying was two sided, Matt."

He finally looked at her, the discomfort clearly visible on his face. Of course. He didn't know how to tell her. She just wasn't for him.

"You deserve better than this," he said softly.

That was a clever way of saying it.

Without arguing she sat up and pulled the sweater over her head. She had some shreds of pride left, damn it.

With all the regal bearing she could muster, she stood, tugged the sweater over her jeans and smoothed her hair. He watched her, a questioning expression on his face.

"Paige." He stood next to her but didn't touch her. He was really over this, she thought bitterly. "I didn't mean to make you cry."

Tapping her jeans pocket to be sure her car keys were still there, she looked at the door. How would she get across this endless room without letting yet another sob give away her shame and hurt?

She would. She just would.

"No need to apologize, Matt." There. Her voice was

under her control. "And I really didn't mean to..."
What? Lead him on? Beg for sex? Respond like a
woman? "Flirt with you."

Squaring her shoulders, she crossed the room and
opened the door without looking back. She was all the
way to her car before she realized she'd left her bra on
the floor.

Well, he could burn it for all she cared. Isn't that what
happens when you play with fire?

Sticking her key into the ignition of her car, she took
one more look at the sun-drenched stone of Auberge du
Soleil. Why *had* she cried? Was she so uncertain and
pathetic that one man's attention reduced her to a weep-
ing mess?

No more, she swore silently. She'd gotten burned,
yes. But she'd be damned if she'd let Walker or Megan
or Matt Camberlane know. He could flip her underwear across the conference room table for all she cared.

Because she would most definitely be seeing him at
their scheduled meeting tomorrow. She didn't know
what made him suddenly pull back from her, but he
couldn't have faked his response to her.

He *wanted* her. Whatever changed his mind...could
be changed back.

And this time everything would be different. She
wanted him just as much, and, damn it, she was going
to get him. Or at least make him miserable wondering
what he'd missed.


Matt lifted up the whisper of white lace that lay
crumpled on the floor, muttering an angry, ugly curse
of frustration.

What the hell did he just do?

He closed his eyes and brought the silky thing to his

face, torturing himself with a deep breath of lavender or roses or some delicate flower. Paige. She had a floral scent all her own. And a taste and feel and sound all her own.

And tears all her own. Damn it. The tears had annihilated him.

At the sight of them, the realization of what their coupling meant to her kicked him square in the face. What was he thinking, seducing an angel? God, she could be a virgin for all he knew. And he'd treated her like any other girl who succumbed to his charm. Some easy conversation, a few quick kisses, then back to his room like another piece of—

He squeezed his eyes shut. He couldn't even think of the expression in relation to this beautiful, real, precious woman. He let her undergarment fall to the chaise longue and dropped his head into his hands. A pain in his chest was just as uncomfortable as the swollen erection that hadn't yet gotten the message that playtime had ended. His blood was nowhere near settled. God only knew what was causing the hurt in his chest.

Could that be his heart?

He blew out another disgusted breath and got up to go to the bathroom.

No doubt he could have handled that situation way better. But the *tears*. The tears just killed him.

The only reason in heaven or hell to have a woman in his life was to have one in his bed. Women were for sexual comfort and gratification. Period. That was the lesson he learned from his miserable marriage to a woman who had used him. He'd vowed he would use them right back.

He stared at his reflection in the bathroom mirror, but only heard the silent promise he'd made two years ago.

Never, *never* again would he lay out his heart like a welcome mat to have high heels dug into it.

He flipped on the cold water tap and stuck his hands under it, hoping it would cool off his heated skin.

Heat caused by Paige's body and mouth and incredibly sexy desire for him.

He hadn't been lying, but she didn't believe him. He meant what he'd said. She deserved better than casual sex.

But casual sex was the only kind he knew.

Surely there was some worthy man, someone who would treat her like the goddess she was. Someone who would wipe her tears and not get freaked out by them. Someone who might even cry with her for how much he loved her.

He splashed a handful of cold water on his face.

Whoa, bud. *That* someone was not Matt Camberlane.

Tomorrow morning he'd go to his office, fax a copy of the contract cancelation to Ashton Estates, then he'd hand the whole event over to someone in his Marketing Department. And then, he'd forget he'd ever met Paige Ashton. Or kissed her. Or ached for her in the most fundamental, frightening way.

The problem was, he thought, as the water sluiced down his cheeks and into the corners of his mouth, he'd never forget her.

But he *had* to. He just had to.

# Four

She sailed past the security guard with the claim of a meeting with Matt Camberlane. But as soon as a no-nonsense, slightly overweight administrative assistant hustled into the lobby of Symphonics, Inc., Paige knew she was about to get the brush-off.

"I'm Eleanor Bradford, Mr. Camberlane's assistant." She held out her hand in greeting but wore a frown and backed it up with a gentle shake of her head. *You don't have an appointment,* her body language screamed.

"Paige Ashton."

Her eyes widened a bit and she leaned back in a not-so-subtle reappraisal. "Are you one of the Ashton Winery family members?"

Fame had its privileges, Paige supposed. "Yes. Mr. Camberlane and I arranged this meeting over the weekend." She gave Eleanor her very best business-school-confident tilt of her head. "He's expecting me."

"He is?" The woman looked unconvinced. No doubt Mr. Camberlane, multizillionaire boy wonder and world-class flirt, had his share of young women with faux appointments. Eleanor was just doing her job as gatekeeper.

Eleanor's expression changed from confusion to understanding. "Oh, I know what happened. You didn't receive the fax I sent this morning."

Oh, yes, she did. "The fax?" Paige worked to sound perplexed.

"I'm afraid Mr. Camberlane had to nullify the contract he'd signed. So that would cancel your meeting today. Why don't you wait here while I go grab a copy for you?"

Paige never changed the expression on her face as her mind whirled with options. "That's a pity." Should she *demand* to see him? No. She wanted the element of surprise on her side. She wanted to see his face when he wasn't expecting her. "Do you mind if I come with you and use the ladies' room, then? It was a long drive from Napa."

Eleanor hesitated a moment, then nodded. "Of course. There's one by my desk." Indicating for Paige to follow her, she leaned closer and added, "I was sorry to hear about your father's, uh, passing."

Paige nodded politely. "Thank you."

"Any progress on the investigation?"

Gossip would buy her access and maybe even time to linger near Matt's office, but she didn't relish the idea of using her father's death and the headlines about the family to get what she wanted. Especially when what she wanted was…a man.

"They're looking at every possible angle," she said, coolly enough to stop the casual interrogation.

Eleanor used a key card to open a door that led to a maze of shoulder-high cubicle walls, giving Paige an occasional glimpse at various techie-types at computers or around small tables having meetings. The Symphonics employees were all as young and hip as the music that blared from various computers and sound systems, most of them wearing the standard Silicon Valley uniform of jeans and slogan-covered T-shirts.

Would Matt be dressed like that? Paige tried to swallow at the thought of seeing him again, refusing to fall back into the doubt and introspection that had kept her awake all night.

She'd made up her mind. She'd thought this thing through. She wasn't backing down. His response to her was real. And her response to him? Oh, that was very, very real.

Real enough for her to want an explanation for his sudden change in behavior. And real enough for her to want more. That's what she wanted. Him. In the most primal, physical way.

Around a corner and through another set of doors, they approached a spacious sitting area surrounded by offices instead of cubicles. While Eleanor ambled over to her L-shaped desk, Paige was drawn to the velvety voice of Sinatra coming from the corner office.

Adrenaline and anticipation sluiced through her veins. That had to be Matt's office. But a feminine chortle of laughter coming from the same place caught Paige off guard.

"The ladies' room is down that hall to your left," Eleanor instructed as she riffled through papers, evidently unfazed by the sound of a woman laughing and Frank Sinatra singing in the middle of a Monday morning. "I'll find that contract by the time you get back."

The hall was in the opposite direction of the office that beckoned her. Ignoring Eleanor's instructions, Paige moved forward, getting a glimpse of the corner of his desk, a large window that faced a pond and trees, and part of a leather sofa that lined one wall.

And what was on that leather sofa stopped Paige cold. From her vantage point, all she could see were two long, bare, gorgeous legs finished off by a pair of slinky cream pumps.

The legs uncrossed and crossed again, accompanied by another throaty laugh.

"I can handle anything, and you know that." One leg slid over the other again, very slowly this time. "Better than anyone."

"I just need you to handle an event, Tessa." The baritone of his voice easily overpowered the soft music, but not the sudden rush of blood in Paige's ears.

"It'll be no problem, Matty." *Matty?* "I'm sure your guests will be happy not to have to stay home and hand out candy to brats all night, anyway. I'll start researching possible venues this morning."

Eleanor turned from her desk and slid her gaze pointedly toward the hall. "Down there, Miss Ashton. To the left."

Was that a warning to run or a reminder that the possible venues no longer included Ashton Estate Winery? Either way, Paige was just seconds and inches away from a most embarrassing encounter. Not only had she defied the fax she'd received at eight that morning and ignored the chilly voice mail message Matt had left her, now she was face-to-face with the competition who'd gotten the job. And by the looks of those flip-flopping legs, the competition who'd get Matt, too.

Turning on her heel, Paige headed toward the ladies' room with enough speed that Eleanor probably thought she was about to have an accident.

Inside, she put both hands on the counter and stared in the mirror. She hadn't seen the woman's face, but did she have to? She'd be tall, blond, svelte, perfect. She had a sexy snicker and legs that could stop traffic.

And now she had Paige's event and a month of attention from "Matty."

Damn.

No, Paige told herself, shaking her head at her own image as if she could rattle some sense into it. Had she worked all night last night and driven all the way down to San Francisco just to be outmaneuvered by a pair of legs?

She wrinkled her nose at herself, trying to see past her too-small chin, too-nondescript eyes, her too-mouse-brown hair, and way-too-boyish figure.

Megan said her face was delicate. Her mother said a small chin is a sign of good breeding. Her hairstylist did her best to add a few highlights to that brown. And her figure? She ran her hands over the apricot knit dress she'd carefully selected because it was professional but definitely feminine.

Her figure certainly didn't seem too boyish to Matt Camberlane when he'd explored it yesterday.

"I'm not giving up," she whispered to her reflection. "I'm not leaving without finding out what spooked him yesterday." She'd do what she had to do to get the answers she wanted, and if she managed to pull in the contract in the process, wonderful. Megan would be delighted. "Ashtons don't give up," she reminded herself.

The door whooshed open and with one glance at the familiar pumps, Paige knew exactly who'd entered.

Okay, not blond. Brunette. But tall, svelte and flawless just the same.

The woman's ebony eyes danced with mirth, and a confident, secret smile played on her lips.

*Keep your friends close and your enemies closer.* Twenty-two years under the tutelage of Spencer Ashton had at least taught her that much.

"Hello," Paige said, turning from the sink. "Do you work here?"

The woman paused on her way into a stall, noticing Paige for the first time. "Yes, I do. I'm Tessa Carpenter. I work in Marketing. And you?"

"I'm Paige Ashton," she said, holding out her hand. "I have a meeting here this morning."

Tessa raised a striking, sculpted brow, as though no one could actually have a meeting at Symphonics that she didn't know about. "With…?"

"Matt Camberlane."

That got her attention. The dark eyes widened and dropped in a quick review. "I just left his office," she announced, then smiled as she stepped toward a stall door. "I think that put him in a better mood than he was in the morning."

"Oh?" Paige turned to the mirror and unsnapped her handbag. "That's funny. He was in a great mood all weekend."

The door froze as Tessa looked at her. "Really."

Paige dabbed on some shiny lip gloss. "Really."

"Where did you see him this weekend?"

"A fund-raiser. Dinner. A picnic." Paige watched Tessa pale ever so slightly. "In fact, we're having lunch this afternoon."

"It's only ten o'clock." Tessa said slowly. "You're kind of early for a lunch meeting."

Paige checked her lips in the mirror. "Yes. I am." Then she snapped her bag closed and headed toward the door, feeling wickedly elated.

Tessa Carpenter and her endless legs were not going to get her down. She had a mission, a goal. She had no idea how, but she was going to march right into that office and let that electricity zing between them again. She wanted that thrill, that delicious, addictive sensation that wound through her when he kissed her, touched her, liquified her whole being. She wanted it and she intended to get it.

With a determined push, she yanked open the door and walked right into Matt Camberlane.

*"Paige?"* Matt had to blink to be sure he wasn't just conjuring her up as he left the mens' room.

She lifted her face toward him and gave him a bright smile. "I'm a few minutes early."

"Early?"

"For our meeting." She lifted her briefcase an inch. "You're going to love these ideas."

He deserved this. He deserved to squirm in front of her. He should have explained things to her, not let her run off making all sorts of wrong assumptions. And then he didn't call her—unless you count a lousy voice mail message with a mumbled excuse about delays in the product launch. Hell, yeah. He deserved to suffer.

Only, he wasn't suffering. Because looking at those innocent eyes, standing in the enclosed hallway close enough to almost drop a kiss on her caramel-colored hair was not suffering. In fact, it was a lot closer to heaven than hell.

Indicating the executive suites with one hand, he said, "My office is this way, Paige."

Even though he wanted to touch her so badly he literally ached, he fought the urge to place a hand on her back as they walked together. He wouldn't touch her. He would not lay a single finger on her body.

Eleanor looked up from her desk and her jaw slackened.

"Hold my calls, please," he instructed her, not taking the time to respond to the surprised look on his assistant's face.

Paige seemed to know exactly where to go, entering his office ahead of him.

"Have a seat." He pulled out one of the guest chairs in front of his desk, somehow not wanting her to sit on the sofa where Tessa Carpenter had just licked her chops over him. Paige wasn't a slink-on-the-leather kind of girl. She was a sit-in-the-straight-back-chair kind of girl.

Wasn't she?

As she sat, the hem of her peachy sweater dress rose just enough to make him question that thought. The silky thigh the move revealed collided with the image of Paige sliding out of her clothes the previous day. His whole lower half threatened to jump up and betray his thoughts. Good God, was he incapable of having a conversation with this woman without getting aroused?

He closed the door and tapped the wall switch that automatically lowered the sound system.

"Don't turn off Frank on my account," she said. "I've been humming 'Under My Skin' for two days."

His reaction to that was definitely above the waist. "You have?"

She turned in the chair to face him. "Just thinking about the VoiceBox launch party makes me hum some great songs."

Well, that explained it. She hadn't received the fax or his message. And even after the way they left things on Sunday afternoon, she showed up for a meeting, all professional and ready to work.

Sitting across from her in the other chair, he took a deep breath. There'd be no hasty, feeble explanations of a product delay now. He had to tell her the truth.

"Paige—"

Before he could speak, she began to spread papers on his desk. "Here's the room layout I worked out."

"Paige, wait."

"No," she shook her head and held up one finger. "You wait. Wait until you see the idea I had for the centerpieces."

He opened his mouth to stop her again, but his gaze fell on the picture of a gray felt hat—Sinatra's trademark—tipped over the corner of a laptop screen. He couldn't help smiling. "Now would you look at that?"

"Oh, that's just something I worked up off the Internet," she assured him. "There'll be a laptop on each table with a different theme that instantly brings to mind the musician. Lips for Mick Jagger, oversize glasses for Elton John."

Unable to resist, he lifted another page and scanned it.

"You did a lot of work yesterday," he said slowly. "I'm impressed."

She didn't respond for a moment as the flush deepened in her cheeks. "I didn't want to just sit around and think."

About what a jerk he was, no doubt. "Paige." He put his hand over hers, loving the slender, smooth feel of it. There went the vow not to touch her. "I canceled the contract and this meeting."

"I know."

She knew? He just stared at her.

"I got your fax and your message. But I really wanted you to see these ideas, so I decided to bend the rules and muscle my way into your office." She gave him a saucy grin. "Pretty good muscling, huh?"

He couldn't fight his own smile as he studied her. "Yeah. Damn good. Muscled your way right past Eleanor, and that's no easy feat."

"Eleanor was a breeze. Now, Tessa, in the bathroom. She was a little more protective of you."

He laughed out loud at that. "She works for me."

"Yes, in Marketing. I know."

"She was here to be briefed—"

"On the product announcement and event. I know."

Still smiling, he leaned back in his chair and let out a little puff of air in defeat. "Is there anything you don't know?"

"I don't know why you got so weird on me yesterday afternoon."

His throat closed up. Not at what she said, but at the brave, straightforward way she said it. He owed this lady an explanation and, more than that, he admired her for seeking it out.

Searching her face, he tried to form the right words. *Your tears freaked me out?* He'd sound like a basket case. *You're too refined and intelligent for me to seduce?* What, he only slept with coarse, classless girls? *You want emotion and I want sex?*

Bingo.

He looked down for one second, then back into those ever-changing eyes. Forget the color, he could just get lost in the shape and size and patience he saw as she waited for his explanation.

"When you cried, Paige, I realized that a...a physical relationship was more meaningful to you than it…than it usually is to me." Geez. He sounded like a cad. "I mean, I generally don't get emotionally involved with the women I…" No better.

He stood suddenly, moving behind his chair to grip the backrest, aware that her gaze never left him. "I…I just sensed that casual sex and you…don't mix well."

She didn't say a word.

He waited a beat, then added, "I respect you."

"Well, that's a shame."

A *shame?* "Pardon me?"

"Because your respect cost me a very important piece of business."

"A piece of— Do you want to have this event at your winery that much?"

She arched a brow. "I want it very much, yes. Enough to get past the awkwardness of a single, unexpected moment where we…lost control." She stood and shuffled the papers on his desk. "But not if it's going to make you so uncomfortable you stutter."

He was not stuttering. Was he?

He slammed a hand over the papers. "Not so fast, Miss Paige Ashton."

She looked up questioningly, a teasing smile at the corner of her lips. "Yes, Matt?"

"I like those ideas."

"I knew you would." She shrugged. "But they're mine. They come with the Ashton Estate Winery locale and my event-planning skills." She tugged at the papers under his hand. "Evidently, you *respect* me too much to get a chance to see them executed."

He couldn't hold back the laugh. "You're muscling again."

Her smile widened, but she kept her attention on the papers, trying to sort them neatly.

"I keep forgetting you're an Ashton."

That earned him a quick look. "And we're fairly adept at getting what we want."

"I see that." He fluttered the sketch of Frankie's felt hat. "Now I'm sorry I canceled that contract."

"I happen to have another one right here." Without missing a beat, she flipped a piece of paper in front of him and produced a pen. "All you have to do is sign."

She had no idea what she was asking him to do. Their attraction was palpable, and not acting on it would take every ounce of control he wasn't sure he had.

"I...I can't."

She leaned close enough to tease him with that dainty, flowery scent. The same aroma that lingered on the silk bra that he'd dropped into his suitcase when he left Auberge.

"Can't?" she asked, holding his gaze with a look so rich with promise and possibilities that it damn near knocked the wind out of him. "I seem to recall you don't know what that word means."

Her smile was pure victory as she handed him a pen.

He could do this.

After Matt gave his keys to the Ritz-Carlton valet, he rounded the back end of his Ferrari to meet Paige, as another valet opened her door.

He repeated his silent mantra, the one he'd started during their two-hour morning meeting about the Voice-Box launch event.

He could do this. He could work on a project with a woman he was wildly attracted to and not seduce her. He could get the benefit of her ideas and business acumen—which was formidable—and he could walk away without having to get the view from on top of her.

He wasn't a teenager crazed by lust-starved hormones.

He made it around the car just in time to see that slinky dress slide up her thighs as she maneuvered out of the low sports car. A demon of an early erection threatened.

Not a teenager? Okay. Then he was an *adult* crazed by lust-starved hormones. But he was also the born competitor. He'd just think of this as one major competition. The brain vs. the body.

Good money was on the…oh, hell.

She gave him a sunny smile. "The Ritz, eh? You're not thinking about checking out their function rooms are you?"

"Not a chance. You won me over this morning." He led her into the lobby toward his favorite luncheon spot, The Terrace. "The event is going to be held on Halloween at Ashton Winery Estate," he assured her. "Your ideas are too good to pass up."

At least, that was the reason he gave himself for signing the contract. Flimsy, but he'd hold on to it.

They were seated at his favorite table on the brick courtyard of The Terrace, secluded among the flowers and trees, and serenaded by the cascade of a giant fountain.

"Walker introduced me to this place," Matt told her after they'd listened to the waiter describe an array of Mediterranean-themed specials. "We used to come here for Sunday brunch when we were in college."

Her eyebrow shot up in disbelief. "Pretty swanky place for a couple of Berkeley students."

"Trust me, we hit the not-so-swanky places the night before." He dropped a linen napkin on his lap. "That was the great thing about Walker. You'd never know his background. He was always really down to earth. But after a week of midterms and all-nighters, he was the first to pull out his wallet and say, 'Matty boy, we need some decent chow.'"

She laughed at his dead-on impression of the serious Walker Ashton.

"And we'd come here and eat like, well, like starving Berkeley students on a trust fund. And he'd always pay." He shook his head in amazement. "Before Walker, I'd never even heard of the Ritz-Carlton."

Paige took a sip of water and regarded him closely. "You didn't talk much about your childhood the other night. Where are your parents?"

Good question, he thought wryly. Where are my parents? "My dad is MIA and has been for as long as I can remember."

She frowned at the idea or the acronym, he didn't know which.

"He left when I was a child and never made too much of an effort to keep in touch." He took a sip of water, making a conscious decision to barrel on with information he shared with few people. "And my mom…well, she's finally settled into a real home for the first time in her life and she seems to be getting her act together." *Seems* being the operative word. "I help her out a lot. She's better when she doesn't have to hold down a job."

This was business, he reminded himself. No need to delve into the gross dysfunctionality of his tiny family. But he could tell by her interested look the subject wasn't going to die.

"What do you mean 'settled into a real home'?"

"One without wheels."

Her frown deepened with genuine confusion. "I don't understand."

Of course not. She'd probably never seen a double-wide trailer park home in her whole life. "Forget about it," he said, sweeping open his menu. "I recommend the monkfish. The seafood is unmatched here."

Her gaze lingered on him for a moment, another question poised on her pretty lips, but then her attention shifted over his shoulder and her expression changed to one of surprise.

He turned to see Walker Ashton headed directly toward them.

"Well, speak of the devil." Matt stood and set his napkin on the table to shake Walker's hand. "I say your name and you appear." Matt frowned. "Or you're following us."

"Hey, Matt." Walker returned the shake, then his dark gaze moved to his cousin. He leaned over and kissed Paige on the cheek. "Seems impossible to pry you two apart lately."

Was that disapproval or accusation in Walker's voice? Matt pointed to one of the empty chairs at the table. "Grab a seat. We haven't even ordered yet."

"For a minute." The chair scraped over the brick floor as Walker pulled it out. "I have a lunch meeting with a new client and then I'm picking up Tamra at two to fly back to South Dakota." He turned to face Paige. "How's the event planning going?"

The pointed question elicited the slightest flush on her cheeks. "Great. We've got a theme, decor, entertainment, a guest list and an invitation design all completed this morning."

"So," Walker looked from one to the other. "Why are you still meeting?"

"Budget," Matt said without thinking.

"Time line," Paige said at the same time, then cleared

her throat and ignored Walker's snort of laughter at the contradiction. "Matt was just telling me how you two used to frequent the brunches here in college."

Walker's grin was slow as his gaze slid to Matt. "Then I guess I should be glad he's bringing you here instead of some of our less respectable hangouts in Oakland."

"Maybe you'll take me to one of those, too, Matt." Her smile was anything but innocent. "I'm always interested in seeing what less than respectable looks like."

Her meaning was not lost on him and by the burn in Walker's stare, it wasn't lost on him, either.

She wasn't doing such a bang-up job of keeping this pure business, he thought. The morning meeting had been filled with longer-than-businesslike glances and a definite sense of play and not work in her quick comebacks.

And she'd looked damn near triumphant when he called the Marketing Department to tell Tessa he'd hired an outside consultant to do the event.

Suddenly Paige pushed her chair back and stood. "Excuse me for a moment, please."

They both stood up as she left the table, their similar heights bringing the two men face-to-face.

"I thought you were doing a good deed." Walker's voice had no humor.

Matt rubbed his chin thoughtfully as he considered a response. "I'm taking a business associate to lunch to discuss an event we're planning. I fail to see how that's a bad deed."

Walker's thick native-American brows knotted and his dark eyes narrowed. "When you bid on her, Matt, you said, 'I'm only doing a good deed.' You felt sorry for her or something."

"That's true." He felt…*something*. Not sorry, but this

wasn't the right time to explain that. "Then I hired her to manage an event. Something she happens to be very good at. Is that a problem?"

"It could be." Walker was far too familiar with Matt's track record for him to easily buy that excuse. Matt had even confided that he had no intention of ever getting serious with a woman again after his divorce; he'd been very clear about his "sex without strings" personal philosophy.

"I don't intend for it to go beyond the boardroom, Walker," he added, lowering his voice and holding his friend's slightly hostile gaze. "You don't have to worry about me."

"I'm not in the least bit worried about you." Walker glanced in the direction where Paige had gone. "I'm worried about my little cousin. She does her best to be tough but…"

"But what?"

"She's got a soft heart."

And soft lips. And soft hair. "I can tell," Matt admitted.

"And she's shy."

*Shy?* Could Walker—or the other Ashtons—not know the same Paige he did? She was definitely not shy. Quiet, thoughtful and intelligent, but not shy. "She's not timid, Walker. She knows how to get what she wants."

"That's just a front," Walker insisted. "She tries to be as in control as her sister Megan, and as shrewd as their mother. But she's tender, not tough. She's…she's not…"

"She's not what?"

"She's not your type."

Now *that* was debatable. "I know what you're trying to say," Matt assured his friend. "You can trust me."

Walker put his hand on Matt's shoulder and gave him

a quick squeeze. They went too far back, had too much history and friendship, for either one to doubt the truth of Matt's promise.

"I know that, Matty boy. I know that." Walker cocked his head toward Paige's empty chair. "Tell her I had to run."

When Walker disappeared into the dining room of The Terrace, Matt caught a glimpse of Paige approaching the table. Her slender hips swayed a bit with each step, her breasts moved just enough to make his mouth water.

She moistened her lips ever so slightly and kept her gaze locked on him.

Matt knew women. And he knew for a fact that this one most definitely had something on her mind other than a time line or a budget.

But he'd made his promise. To himself. And, more important, to his friend.

# Five

Paige had to give him credit. Matt was doing everything humanly possible to keep their interaction strictly business. Or at least not personal.

And hadn't she planned to do the same thing on their first date just a few nights ago? She'd failed miserably…and he would, too.

For one thing, their "meeting" had started at ten, then continued on through a two-hour lunch, and showed no sign of ending now that they were strolling through Ghirardelli Square like a couple of tourists.

Like a *couple.* Period.

It was unspoken that they didn't want the "meeting" to end. He'd suggested they drive over to the square after lunch to soak in the incredible autumn California day, and she hadn't argued. The sun warmed the golden brick pavement of the sprawling park, and their easy conversation and comfortable silences warmed her heart. Nothing intimate, nothing personal. But not exactly business, either.

"I haven't been here for years," Paige said as they passed the historic chocolate factory. "I forgot how quaint and inviting this place is."

"It's touristy," he noted. "But there's a reason the tourists like it."

They entered a tree-lined plaza, pausing at a storefront to admire the hand-blown glass in the window.

"We can't leave the square without making a wish," Matt said suddenly, taking her hand. "Let's visit Andrea."

Her fingers curled around his much stronger ones. Oh, yes. This was feeling more like a date and less like a meeting every minute. "Andrea?"

"The mermaid of the fountain." He tugged her toward the massive sculpture of two mermaids nursing their babies and surrounded by a pool of sun-drenched water. "Gotta make a wish."

He dug into his pants pocket and pulled out a handful of change. "Pick a lucky one," he told her.

She plucked a shiny penny from the group, and he took another. As they approached the gray slate steps that surrounded the pool, he dipped his head close to her.

"Andrea listens, you know. So be sure you wish for something good."

She grinned and flipped the penny toward the water. "I know what I want." *I wish Matt would kiss me.* It hit with a tiny splash.

"Wow. You sure do know what you want," Matt noted. "I generally have to think about it for a minute."

"This wish didn't take any thought at all," she said, squinting in the sun as she looked up at him. "I know exactly what I want."

"You know what they say."

"What do they say?"

"Be careful what you wish for." With that, he arced his penny in a perfect curve shot.

The water rippled as his coin drifted to meet the coppery cluster at the bottom.

"What did you wish for?" she asked.

He gave her a lopsided grin that made her insides ripple just like the pool. "You tell me first," he said.

"Doesn't that mean my wish won't come true?"

He considered that as they found an empty bench tucked under the branches of a gnarly shade tree, the leaves already beginning to take on the golden hue of October. "I'm not sure how strict Andrea is about revealing your wishes," he said as they sat.

"Then I don't want to risk it," Paige laughed. "I really want this wish to come true."

He crossed his long legs and draped an arm across the back of the bench. Not exactly touching her but not *strictly* professional, either.

"Why don't I guess?" he suggested. "Then technically you really haven't told me."

She smiled, feeling coy and flirtatious. Not a sensation Paige Ashton was used to, but one that sure sent a few lovely tingles through her. "Okay. You get three guesses."

He laughed. "Oh, there are rules, now. Hmm. Okay. Let me guess." He studied the fountain in front of them, then said, "You wished for a flawlessly executed, well-attended, completely successful launch party for VoiceBox."

She just stared at him. Was he that unromantic? "I don't have to wish for that. I'll make that happen without the help of any mermaids or wishes."

"Touché." He thought for a moment. "I know. You covered all your bases. You wished for happiness and a lifetime of contentment."

She shook her head. "I wouldn't want to strain Andrea's powers with anything that monumental. My wish was simple. And it was nothing I could control. Someone else has to make it happen."

"You want all your family problems to go away."

Oh, God. That's what she should have wished for, she thought guiltily. He wasn't even thinking about a kiss, and she shouldn't have wasted her penny on something so frivolous when there were real problems in her life.

She managed to nod. "Yes, that's it. My family."

"Is there anything I can do?" he asked.

That he could do? "Not unless you want to step into a beehive of distrust, accusation, blackmail and infidelity."

"That sounds like my family," he said with a quick laugh. "On a much smaller scale and without the blackmail, of course."

Something twisted in her heart at the lack of judgment in his tone. "I guess everyone has their skeletons," she admitted.

"Yeah, in the closet. Your family has them on the front page of the business section and weekly tabloids."

Wasn't that the ugly truth? "Are you sure you still want to hold your event at the Winery?"

"I most certainly do," he assured her. "And my offer of help stands. Not that I can do anything to relieve the situation other than listen and offer sympathy."

A sigh escaped her lips when he said that. "You better watch it, Matt," she warned. "That's pretty sensitive talk for a tough, competitive entrepreneur like you."

He winked at her. "Just trying to make your wish come true."

*Then kiss me.*

For a dizzying second, he looked as though he might. His lips were parted, the pupils dilated against his steel-gray eyes. Then he looked back at the fountain.

"I don't think there's much you can do as far as my family is concerned," she said quickly. "I'm planning to go up to Louret Vineyards tomorrow. It's time for another visit with my half sisters and another attempt at fence mending."

"Want some company?"

She leaned back and gave him a surprised look. "You want to go up to Louret? With me?"

"Sure. I can take a day off tomorrow, and I'd love to take a drive up there. I've heard Louret's a magnificent vineyard."

"The vineyard is breathtaking, but the family…"

"Not so breathtaking?"

She smiled at the way he tried to make her comfortable with a decidedly uncomfortable subject. "My half siblings are very, very angry at my father, as you can imagine, and, by association, at my brother and sister and cousins and me. My father virtually abandoned those children when he married my mother."

"I'd heard that from Walker."

"They think I'm taking his side."

"Are you?"

She shook her head vehemently. "I told you the other night, I don't take sides. I walk a tightrope right down the middle."

"That's a dangerous place, Paige," he said, his fingers grazing her shoulders. "If you fall, you can get hurt."

Her lips curled in a rueful smile. "I have great balance."

"What do you hope to accomplish tomorrow?"

She shrugged, liking that his fingers had settled on her shoulder. Wanting to fold into his substantial body for a reassuring hug. "I just want to visit. To show them that, well, we're family. We have our differences, but we should stick together."

"What kind of differences?"

"My father's will, for one thing."

"Walker told me they are contesting it."

"They might." She picked up a leaf that had fallen on the bench and studied it. "And they have a fairly compelling reason to do that. As you've no doubt read in those papers and tabloids, my father's marriage to their mother was…not legal. He never divorced his first wife."

"Yes, I read about that."

"We're a mess," she said with an apologetic laugh, flicking the leaf into the air. "Look up dysfunctional and you'll see the Ashton Family Album in the dictionary."

He shook his head. "Like I said, no different from other families, just on a grander scale. Maybe your visit would be more comfortable—and effective—if you have company. Less like an investigation and more like a social call. I'd love to go with you."

"Why would you do that?"

He leaned closer. "So I can get my wish."

Her heart tumbled right off that tightrope she'd just mentioned and splattered in her tummy. "Okay, tell me. What did you wish for?"

He dipped his head so close to hers that she could feel the warmth of his skin. "I can't tell you. Then it might not come true."

"*Can't* again, huh?" She pulled back enough to give him a teasing grin. "You're starting to sound like a broken record."

Megan looked up from her desk with a mock scowl, held her wrist in the air, and tapped one manicured fingernail on the face of her watch.

"The meeting at Symphonics ran late," Paige explained as she breezed in. "Anything earth-shattering happen while I was gone?"

"You tell me," Megan said pointedly. "You're the one who spent, oh, eight hours with one client."

Eight lovely hours. Paige dropped into the chair across from Megan's desk and managed not to purr with sheer delight. "We had a lot to cover."

"Such as?"

"Seating arrangements, invitations, decorations, audio-visual, guest list." And some wish making.

"Uh-huh." Megan flipped her long blond hair over her shoulder and leaned her elbows on the desk. "And what else?"

"Time line, budget, music—"

"Did he kiss you?"

Paige let her jaw drop in an effort to look suitably indignant. "Of course not."

"Did you kiss him?"

"Megan! I don't make a habit of kissing clients."

"I did." Megan winked. "Just once, though."

Hopefully, that signaled a change in subject. "Did you and Simon find the perfect crib in Calistoga yesterday?"

"He's really gorgeous."

The statement threw her. "Your husband? Yes, he's a god."

"No, I mean, yes, he is a god. But I'm not talking

about Simon, sweetie, and you know it." Megan leaned back and rubbed her belly as she regarded her sister. "Matt Camberlane qualifies as irresistible."

"I can resist." Yeah, right. She'd really resisted him in his room at Auberge. She practically stripped before he'd gotten the door closed. And left half her underwear as a souvenir.

"I've heard he's a real player, too, since his divorce."

"His divorce?" Her heart plummeted in disappointment. A player? She could believe that. But he'd never mentioned a previous marriage. "He didn't tell me he was divorced."

"Why would he? I thought you were just doing budgets, invitations and seating arrangements." Megan's voice held just enough of a tease to take the sting out of the accusation.

"We were. And I swear there was no lip contact today." True enough. *Today* there hadn't been. "Just a handshake as we made plans for tomorrow."

Megan's eyebrows shot up. "Another meeting?"

"Can you spare me?" Paige asked. "I really want to go up to Louret."

"So you said at breakfast yesterday. And do your plans include taking Matt Camberlane to Louret?"

Paige nodded, moving her gaze to the bay window behind Megan's desk and making a point of studying the late afternoon shadows on the estate grounds.

"Why?" Without looking, she could feel Megan's stare burning her. "What does that have to do with the Halloween product launch party we're doing for Symphonics?"

"Well…" Paige plucked at an imaginary thread on her dress. "Nothing."

Their gazes finally met as Megan waited for an explanation.

"He offered to come with me. To make it comfortable, more social and less like a showdown. I can take him to the tasting room and just chat with Jillian."

"No, you can't."

More disappointment. "Megan, we don't have any events scheduled for tomorrow. I don't need to be here."

"Louret's tasting room is closed on Tuesdays."

"Oh, well, that's okay. Jillian usually spends her days off at The Vines, so I'll just visit with her and Mercedes, if she's around."

"Anna Sheridan is staying there," Megan said, referring to the woman who'd assumed custody of baby Jack, the result of their father's last fling.

Jack's mother had died shortly after giving birth, but her sister, Anna, had been welcomed into the home of Caroline and Lucas Sheppard. That act alone proved to Paige that Caroline, Spencer Ashton's second wife, had plenty of class.

"I'd really like to meet the little guy," Paige admitted. "Jillian told me he's cute as a button."

Megan rubbed her tummy. "I saw a picture of him. He's divine. Makes me want a boy."

"As if it matters. With you and Simon as parents, he or she will be dazzling, smart and the control freak from hell."

Megan laughed. "I've been better lately, don't you think?"

"Yep. Raging morning sickness is the first thing to slow you down in your life."

"It's not just that. I want to concentrate on Simon. I'm letting you manage the whole Symphonics thing, aren't I?"

"Well, Matt has his hands all over it, too."

"Just so he doesn't have his hands all over you, little sister."

Heat coursed through her at the thought.

"Or has he already?" There was no tease in Megan's accusation this time.

Paige said nothing, avoiding her sister's probing gaze.

"You slept with him?" Megan asked, shocked.

"No!" That, at least was the truth. The hands-all-over-her part, well. He had done that. And would again, if Paige had her way. "I did not sleep with him."

The only sound was the ticking brass clock on Megan's desk.

"Yet," Paige added quietly.

Megan searched her face with a plea in her eyes. "Paige, don't do anything stupid."

A burst of anger propelled her from the chair. "Why is it when anyone else in this family falls into *lust,* it's fine. With baby Paige, it's stupid. I'm twenty-two, Meg. I'm not a virgin." Paige folded her arms and looked down at Megan. "The guy melts my bones. I want him."

Megan sighed as the echoes of Paige's admission hung in the room. "I'd be a hypocrite if I told you I don't know how good it feels to want someone who melts your bones. I still feel it every time Simon looks at me."

"I can feel it when the two of you are in the same room."

"Yeah," she said wistfully. "It's nice, this love stuff. But, Paige, I don't think Matt Camberlane has 'love stuff' in mind. Walker told me he was burned by his wife and is definitely committed to not being committed, if you get my drift."

Great. Now Megan and Walker were discussing her love life. Or sex life, as the case may be. "Listen, I don't want love, or even a commitment, Meg." A sly smile lifted Paige's lips. "I just want that bone-melting business again."

"Again?"

"Well, things got a little heated on Sunday. But…we stopped." He stopped. But some things couldn't be shared. Even with a sister.

"Just be careful, sweetie. I don't want you to end up with a broken heart."

With a sudden rush of affection, Paige came around the desk, dipping down to hug Megan. "I won't," she promised. "And you know what? This 'love stuff' sure agrees with you."

"Nah." Megan smiled ruefully. "I'm still a control freak, Paige. And if anybody hurts my little sister, I'll…I'll—"

"Sic Simon on him?"

"And Walker and Trace," she promised.

"I'll be fine," Paige assured her. "And you're okay with my being gone tomorrow?"

Megan nodded. "Things are under control in the Event Planning Department. You see what you can do with the family problems."

"I will."

"And don't let your bones melt too easily, Paige."

Paige just laughed. Too late for that. She was a puddle.

# Six

In the late-morning light, the twenty-something-thousand-square-foot mansion of Ashton Estate Wineries looked gilded by the sun. The dark cream-colored stone took on a tawny, golden tinge that reminded Matt of the honey-toned streaks in Paige Ashton's hair.

With a quick shake of his head, Matt erased the thought and parked in the circular drive.

He'd done a magnificent job of staying on the phone for the whole hour and fifteen minutes it took him to drive up from San Mateo. He'd participated in a product development conference call, listened to his CFO wax eloquent about VoiceBox preorders, and convinced the president of one of the world's largest retailers to rearrange four thousand stores to prominently feature the product before Christmas.

He'd *worked*. He refused to buckle under the temptation to slide Ol' Blue Eyes into the CD player and let his mind wander…and reconsider just why he'd made this unorthodox offer in the first place.

He'd already decided, and there was nothing he hated more than second guessing a decision.

He'd decided to accompany Paige to visit her half siblings for one simple reason: to up the ante. To raise the stakes. What good was a little body vs. brain challenge if it was too easy? If he was really going to win a battle with his libido, then he had to immerse himself in her world and torture his senses with proximity.

Then he could walk away after the VoiceBox launch party, shake her hand and say, "Great working with you, Paige." And wouldn't that be something?

Yeah. Something *stupid.*

But it wasn't stupid to prove to himself that he could indeed have a platonic relationship with a woman who charged him sexually. Especially when he sensed the same electrical impulses arced through her body, too.

He could do it. He'd promised Walker, and he'd promised himself. He could work with her and even develop a friendship with her, but he wouldn't risk seeing those tears again. Regardless of how she managed to lean a little too close, and hold their eye contact a little too long.

Before he could open the driver's door, Paige emerged from the shadow of the overhang that ran along the east wing of the estate. As she stepped into the sunshine, he just gave in and admired her. She wore pale yellow from top to toe—reminding him of sweet creamery butter that could, with one warm touch, melt in his hands.

A line from one of his favorite songs flashed in Matt's head. Something about only you beneath the moon…and under the sun.

With a quick wave she indicated for him to stay in

the car as she approached, but he climbed out and took another appreciative glance at the way her silk trousers hugged her narrow hips, and still another glimpse at the tempting curves under the designer sweater.

"Morning, sunshine." He dug his hands into his pockets to keep from embracing her.

"Hi, Matt." Her smile was as blinding as the California rays that warmed them. "All ready to do your good deed for the day?"

He slipped his arm around her shoulder. He couldn't help it. It was natural. Casual. Impossible. "If that's how you want to classify this trip. I've never been to Louret Vineyards, so I'm looking forward to the tour and tasting."

She dipped out of his grasp gracefully and let him open the passenger door for her. "But you won't today, I'm afraid."

"No?"

"The tasting room's closed on Tuesdays, so the visit is purely social." She slid into the car and gave him another radiant smile. "You don't mind, do you?"

Not if she beamed at him like that all day. "No problem. I'm looking forward to meeting this side of the family."

"I just hope everyone behaves."

He picked up that thread of conversation as he climbed in and started the car. "They are expecting you, correct?"

"I spoke with Jillian, my half sister, last night. She runs the tasting room—she's a wine genius. But today is like a Sunday to her, when the tasting room is closed. However, she promised she'd be spending the day with her stepdaughter, Rachel, at The Vines and welcomed the visit."

"The Vines. That's the house, correct?"

"Yes. It's a short drive from the winery. We'll just stay at the house, if you don't mind. If we go over to the winery, we're sure to run into Cole. He manages the vineyard. And Eli would be there—he's head wine-maker."

"Not willing to face them yet?"

A whisper of a sigh escaped her lips. "Jillian has been the most levelheaded during all of this, the one, I think, who shares my goal to somehow bring this hor-rible chapter in our lives to a close. So I'd rather meet with a like mind."

"And what about Mercedes, her older sister?" He'd read enough in the papers to know the recently wed and newly pregnant Mercedes harbored no deep love for the father who abandoned her.

"Well, it's hard to say." She placed her handbag on the floor of the car and repositioned herself in the deep bucket seat. "We might see Mercedes. And Caroline Sheppard, their mother. But I can't make any promises about how warmly they will treat us."

"Will Jillian tell them you're coming up?"

She nodded. "Yes, she said she'd grease the skids."

"Surely none of them hold you accountable for what your father did while he was alive." He glanced at the endless rolling hills of the Ashton Estate, over the acres of recently harvested vineyards famous for producing a fortune in sparkling wines. Spencer Ashton had built a magnificent showpiece out of the Lattimer property he'd won in his divorce from Caroline, and Matt had no doubt her children were bitter about that especially when the vineyard and estate had been given back to him by Caroline's grandfather. But could they blame the offspring from his next marriage?

"Not accountable, no," she agreed. "But the rivalry they feel is real, and, as I told you, not entirely unjustified.

And they are furious—especially Eli and Cole—that my father left them out of his will. And, of course, once they learned that their parents' marriage was not really legal, since my father hadn't divorced his first wife in Nebraska, then the very future of the Ashton Estate became part of the issue."

"Are they pursuing the legality of the ownership of the estate, too?"

"Not at the moment. They are concentrating on the will. But if it can't be overturned, then who knows what could happen?" She shook her head with a rueful smile. "Like I said, dysfunctional is our middle name. Don't forget we're in the middle of a murder investigation, too."

"Any news? Real news, I mean, not what they repeat in the local media every chance they get."

She looked skyward in mock disgust of the media. "As far as suspects, no. Grant, another of my half siblings, was held for questioning, but he had an alibi."

Walker had told him very little about Grant. "He's from your father's first marriage, in Nebraska?"

"Yes, Grant and Grace are Dad's twins by Sally Barnett, who died before my parents were married. I don't have a clue where Grace is, but Grant arrived in California almost a year ago, in January, after he'd discovered that his father was Spencer Ashton."

"According to the papers, he was cleared by Anna… Sheridan, is it? Who is somehow related to your father's…latest child?" A wry smile tipped Matt's lips as he glanced across the console at Paige. "You better fill me in so I don't accidentally offend anyone."

She laughed. "I doubt they offend easily, but of course I'll tell you. Anna Sheridan is the sister of Alyssa Sheridan, who was my father's last, uh, mistress. Alyssa died shortly after their baby was born, about two years ago. Anna is raising Jack and is staying at The Vines to escape the media glare."

"And she was Grant's alibi?"

"Yes, Anna was with Grant the night of the murder, so he was cleared by the police. And now, as you know, they are focusing on the blackmail leads." Her voice dropped a bit. "But getting nowhere."

"Do you have any personal theories about what happened?"

She shook her head. "You know, a lot of people hated my father. Within my family and outside of it. I mean, I loved him and tried to see him in the best possible light, but even that wasn't easy at times."

He heard the pain that caught in her throat. "You're doing the right thing to try and mend the fences, Paige. There's nothing you can do about the past, but plenty you can do about the future."

She smiled gratefully at the words. "I'm just one voice. And the youngest, at that," she laughed quickly. "Unless you count little Jack. I doubt he gets a vote."

"Will Jack be at the house today?"

She shrugged. "I hope so. I've wanted to meet him for a long time. Of course, I'm not sure how I'll feel about a child who is…my brother."

He gave her a surprised look. "Why's that? I'm sure you'd be a terrific big sister."

She didn't answer for a moment as she gazed out the window. "I don't know. He'll be…a constant reminder of my father's inability to…"

Matt's chest tightened at her words. Spencer Ashton was another man who couldn't win the body vs. brain challenge. "To control himself?" he finished for her.

"That's one diplomatic way of putting it."

"What matters, Paige, is how you handle the situation," he told her, placing a comforting hand over hers. "You can't control how the other members of your family think and act—but you can control how you respond to them. And by going there to extend the proverbial olive branch, I think you're doing the right thing."

He took his eyes off the road just long enough to see the warmth back in her gaze. "Thanks, Matt. Spoken like a real friend."

A friend. Exactly what he wanted to be. "Hey, I'm happy to help you out by coming with you on the mission."

She narrowed her eyes teasingly. "I thought this had something do with getting your wish."

"That, too," he assured her. And just to up the ante a little bit more, he weaved his fingers through hers and held her hand until he had to shift gears.

When Jillian Ashton-Benedict descended the winding staircase into the foyer of The Vines to greet them, Paige was struck once again by how lovely her half sister was. Tall, slender and as graceful as her mother, Caroline, Jillian gave Paige a sense of reassurance and alliance that she'd never felt in the presence of her other half siblings.

Perhaps it was because Paige was the youngest in her family and Jillian was the youngest in hers. As the "babies" they tried harder.

"Hello, Paige. It's so good to see you." Jillian reached out to take both of Paige's hands, erasing the awkward question of whether they would hug like sisters or shake hands like casual acquaintances.

"This is Matt Camberlane," Paige said quickly. She'd mentioned that Matt would be with her when she'd chatted with Jillian last night. If her half sister recognized the entrepreneur's well-known name, or if she was intrigued by the relationship between them, she was far too ladylike to let on. This was due, no doubt, to the fine influence of Caroline Sheppard, who, Paige sadly had to admit, landed a few steps higher on the class ladder than her own mother, Lilah.

"It's a pleasure to meet you, Matt," Jillian said warmly, shaking his hand. "I'm so glad you could come." She guided them past the stairs into the formal living room, an oversize room filled with antiques but just as cheerful and welcoming as the whole French country-style home.

"I hope you'll have the opportunity to meet my stepdaughter, Rachel," Jillian said. "My mother has taken her down to the stables to ride this morning, but they'll be back for lunch. Can you join us?"

Did Caroline *want* her to? Certainly Paige's mother would never have extended an invitation to a member of her husband's "other family" for lunch. The memory of how Lilah practically threw Mercedes and Jillian out of their house when they'd made a sympathy call after her father had died still burned in Paige's mind. At the time Paige had been so upset over the murder and loss of her father, that she hadn't done anything to stop her mother's over-the-top reaction.

But the scene remained vivid in her memory, and inwardly Paige cringed with embarrassment. Yet here was Jillian, five months later, graciously inviting her to lunch.

"We can do that," Matt offered, taking the responsibility from Paige's shoulders. As they sat on a pale celery-green silk sofa, she flashed him a grateful look for the support.

"Yes, that would be lovely," Paige agreed. "We don't want to be a bother."

Jillian waved a hand and took a seat in a chair directly across from Paige. "Not at all. It's a gorgeous day. We'll have lunch on the lanai. Mercedes isn't here today, but

I'm sure Anna can join us after she gets Jack down for a nap. Grant usually stops in the house midday."

"And Cole and Eli?" Paige's stomach tightened at the possibility of having lunch with the half brothers who hated her.

"They are busy at the winery," Jillian said quickly.

"Have they changed their minds about contesting the will?" Paige asked, deciding it was better to have the issue in the open, rather than dancing around what they were all thinking.

Jillian shrugged a narrow shoulder, and a burst of hope spurted through Paige. "Everything is in limbo, as you know, while the police try to solve this murder. Until they do, the will is in probate and contesting it is a moot point."

Paige nodded slowly. Did that mean they might not contest the will? She wasn't sure how far to push the point. "So, otherwise, how are your brothers doing?"

"This is a difficult time for everyone," Jillian said. "Eli and Cole have both found love and a sense of peace in their lives, and for that I am eternally grateful."

"But they aren't at peace where their father is concerned," Paige suggested.

"Lucas Sheppard is our father," Jillian responded, the first hint of an edge in her voice. "In every way but name."

"I know he is," Paige said. Everyone knew her father had refused to let Lucas adopt Spencer's four children. For no reason, as far as Paige could figure out, other than spite. Spencer certainly didn't care about them—he never spoke to them, saw them or showed any interest in their lives after he left Caroline and married Lilah.

Another wave of distaste rolled through Paige, as she felt nothing but shame for the mistakes and bad judgment made by some of the people she truly loved.

"And Mercedes?" she asked, thinking of the luncheon she'd shared with Mercedes over a month ago. At the time, the woman had been tight with bitterness, but she'd since married and progressed nicely with her pregnancy. "How is she feeling?"

Jillian brightened. "She's not throwing up anymore. How about Megan?"

"Better, but not completely out of the nausea stage."

"Well, hello there, buddy," Matt's sudden greeting pulled Paige's attention to the entryway.

A wild tuft of red hair, chubby cheeks and bright green—Ashton green—eyes stared at the three of them.

Paige's heart clutched as she stared right back, mesmerized by the sweet face and the expression of pure innocence on his face. Baby Jack.

Her little brother.

"Come on in, honey," Jillian encouraged him. "Where'd Aunt Anna go to?"

He pointed in the general direction of the door. "Bwawy."

"She's in the library?" Jillian stood and took his hand to walk him into the living room. "It's all right. Come and meet some special people."

Matt reached out for an easy high-five. "Hey, little dude. How's it goin'?"

But Paige was ridiculously paralyzed, her heart suddenly thumping wildly in her chest. She'd never dreamed meeting any man under three feet tall could do this to her, but Jack Sheridan was her brother. Her blood. Her father's child.

And all she wanted to do, she realized with a shock, was scoop him up into her arms and cover his dear little face with wet, warm kisses.

"This is Paige and Matt," Jillian said as she urged him closer. "Can you say hello?"

His smile was pure charm. Oh God, Paige thought with a silent gasp. He's Spencer. At least when her father wanted to turn on the charm, that was the smile the recipient got. Charm had been her father's most effective weapon.

Jack gave her a shaky wave, but held his hand up in front of Matt. "Again! Again!" He smacked Matt's hand several times, then let out a cascade of childish giggles.

Without a moment's hesitation, Paige reached out both arms. "Can I have a hug, Jack?"

"Hug," he repeated, then glanced to Jillian, obviously a little unsure of the strange arms beseeching him.

"You can give Paige a hug," Jillian said, tapping his back to send him in Paige's direction. "She's your—"

For a moment the room was silent, and Jillian froze, obviously unsure of how to describe their odd relationship to a two-year-old.

"My Pay!" Jack exclaimed, an approximation of Paige's name.

"Yes!" Paige chuckled at the sound, her eyes filling with moisture. "I'm your Paige. Now can I have a hug?"

He toddled to her and tentatively entered the arms she held out. Paige folded him to her chest, inhaling his sweet little-boy smell and dropping a kiss on the red curls.

"Hello, Jack," she whispered against the lump that formed in her throat. "I hope we'll be great friends."

The child pulled back to look at her, his grass-green eyes wide and wary. Paige searched his face, seeing the earliest signs of some powerful family traits even in his baby face. But it was his eyes that nearly did her in.

No one could look at this child and wonder whose blood ran in his veins. He was an Ashton, a living, breathing reminder of the sins of her father.

And yet he was also her brother.

His little mouth tipped up in a shy smile. "Pay?"

She couldn't help laughing a little. "You can call me Pay, honey." She pulled him closer and planted another kiss on his head, lifting her gaze to meet Matt's as she did.

And it suddenly dawned on her that the game she was trying to play with Matt—the game of seduction and sex—was no different from the one that had caused this child. Of course, there was no adultery involved. But still.

There was no commitment, either.

Could she live with that?

As the morning moved into early afternoon, an ever-changing cast of characters continually transformed the atmosphere of the room. Paige didn't have an opportunity to consider the troubling questions that ricocheted through her head when she looked at Matt, nor did she have time to analyze all the dynamics of the various personalities at play.

She'd save that—and her uncertainties about Matt—to mull over later.

Shortly after Jack made his appearance, Anna Sheridan had come in search of him. A petite, well-dressed woman in her midthirties, Paige immediately noticed how protective she was of her nephew. Just the fact that she'd sought refuge for Spencer Ashton's child in the home of his former wife showed a woman who would face anything to shield her child—or, in this case, her nephew.

And when Caroline Sheppard had entered the room a little while later, the ambiance had taken yet another change. Paige felt her back go ramrod straight and her jaw clench as she stood to greet her father's former wife.

Would Caroline be icy, neutral or warm? Within minutes Paige knew. With a twinge of envy and admiration, she realized that Caroline Lattimer Ashton Sheppard was the real deal.

From the moment she'd arrived, holding the hand of a pigtailed, brown-eyed imp named Rachel who did little more than gaze at Jillian with unadulterated adoration, Caroline made them welcome.

With just her occasional touch, her easy smile, her obvious contentment with her life, Caroline managed to convey that she had no regrets for how her life had turned out. And, even more, their conversation led Paige to believe that she didn't blame anyone but Spencer for the trauma and drama inflicted on both families.

They enjoyed a leisurely and delicious lunch, served on the lanai that overlooked the rustic carriage house and stables and the gently sloping acres of some of the most sensational Pinot Noir, Merlot, Cab and Petite Verdot grapes in Napa Valley.

Of course, they tasted some of those wines with lunch, and Jillian impressed them all with her in-depth knowledge and insights. They spoke the language of vintner families: harvests, bouquets, vintages and trends, the issues facing the family having been covered with Jillian and Caroline in the living room.

And just to confuse her further, Matt was the ideal guest—entertaining, interested and remarkably adept at positioning himself at her side exactly as a friend, not a boyfriend, would.

When Grant Ashton arrived, the atmosphere of the little gathering suddenly changed again and Paige knew that family business was about to go on the lunch menu.

After a round of introductions and greetings, the large and rugged man pulled out the chair closest to Anna and locked a blue-eyed gaze on Paige. "Do Cole and Eli know you're here?"

Jillian answered first. "They're too busy to come over."

That could be true, Paige told herself. Although much of the harvest had been completed by the end of September, many of the red grapes grown here would ripen this month. They could be busy in the winery. Or unwilling to break bread with the enemy.

"I was just over there," Grant said, tossing a look over his shoulder in the direction of the winery. "Not too much going on right now."

"Whatever their reason," Paige said, holding his direct gaze, "I'm grateful to be so welcome here."

Grant nodded slowly before turning to Anna, when the lines around his eyes crinkled in a warm smile. "Where's Jack?"

"I just put him down for a nap in the guest room," she told him, her return look just as fond. "But it required a promise that you'd wake him up the minute you got home."

Home? Did Grant Ashton, the down-to-earth farmer from Nebraska who'd stormed into California demanding to know his real father, consider Louret Vineyards home? Did Anna?

They weren't living at the house but staying in the cottage and carriage house on the property. Yet they did seem rather settled.

"I'll get him when he calls," Grant promised, shaking his head to decline an offer of wine that Jillian made. Again he directed his attention to Paige. "Any news on the investigation?"

No tiptoeing for this big man.

"Nothing concrete," she said. "The detectives are trying to trail some evidence of blackmail."

He snorted a little and threw a glance at Anna. "Probably a lot of opportunity for that in the old man's past."

Paige swallowed as an uncomfortable silence fell over the lanai. "Yes," she finally said, looking down at her lap. "I'm sure there is."

"Hey," Grant's voice pulled her gaze back up to his. "Whatever he was, it sure isn't something his kids need to take the blame for."

For a moment she couldn't speak. Here was yet another half brother touching her heart. For one wild, insane moment, Paige wondered what it could be like if all these families—all these smart, talented, ambitious and dynamic offspring of one man—could actually live in some semblance of peace.

Was that too much to ask?

Paige gave him a smile of genuine warmth. "I appreciate that, Grant."

With a barely noticeable sigh, Caroline stood and excused herself, and suddenly the impromptu lunch party came to an end. As Paige pushed her chair back, she reached down to pick up her handbag and happened to take a quick glance under the table.

In that flash of a second, she could have sworn she saw Anna's tiny hand enclosed in the much bigger one of Grant Ashton.

# Seven

**"I** don't want to go home."

Matt gave Paige a questioning look as he pulled onto the main road and exited The Vines. "Okay. Where do you want to go?"

Your house. Your arms. Your bed. "I just don't feel like facing my family. They'll expect a full accounting on the day."

That was the truth. She didn't really want to go to his house—oh, yes she did—but the thought of returning to the estate to be interrogated by her mother and Trace was utterly unappealing. And no doubt Megan would want a postmortem.

He tapped the breaks and studied her for a moment, the rumble of the Ferrari engine vibrating the whole car. "I don't expect you can put that debriefing off for too long."

No, she couldn't. And what would she tell them?

That Caroline was a genuine lady who was not at all interested in unearthing the misery of her first marriage by contesting the will or the illegal divorce settlement. That Eli and Cole hadn't changed their adamant stance and wouldn't back down. That Jillian was a fair thinker who not only accepted the olive branch of peace but offered one of her own. That Anna Sheridan was a lovely woman—certainly Grant thought so—and that their adorable baby brother was a mirror image of their father who would be a constant reminder of Spencer's lack of morals.

Yes, she would tell them all that. Later. Tomorrow.

But she didn't want to leave the company of Matt Camberlane. Nor did she want to be alone to question the rightness or wrongness of their obvious attraction. She didn't want to shake his hand and say, "Goodbye, thank you, we'll be in touch."

But she didn't want to be the same morals-free, pleasure-seeking, risk-taking person that her father was, either.

"It's the curse of the fair-minded person," she mused aloud.

"Excuse me?" He pulled onto the main highway, headed south toward the estate.

"I can always see both sides of an argument. It's like living hell, sometimes," she admitted with a laugh. "There are two sides to every story, at least two ways to consider something. I can see both, which makes me feel horribly wishy-washy at times."

"Or balanced," he offered with a quick smile.

One thing she didn't feel when he smiled at her that way—balanced. She felt woefully *unbalanced*.

"So where do you want to go?" he asked.

"Home."

He chuckled. "You will have to make up your mind eventually."

"Where do you want to go?" she countered.

He thought for a moment. "Home."

Hers…or his? The idea of going to his house made every nerve ending in her body sing in anticipation. "Home," she repeated slowly. "You mean…my home."

He shot her an innocent look. "Of course."

She nodded in agreement, and while they drove the half hour to the Ashton Estate, they were comfortably quiet. He slid a dreamy Sinatra CD into the sound system, and she closed her eyes and got lost in the music.

The romantic, soulful music of a sexy man that put all sorts of romantic, soulful and sexy thoughts into her head.

She peeked at Matt from under her lashes. His lips moved slightly with the lyrics. The same delicious, demanding lips that had covered her mouth, sucked her tongue, tasted her breasts.

Fire shot through her.

One hand on the gearshift, his long, masculine fingers casually tapped in time to the song. No, he was playing the imaginary keys of a piano, she realized. With the same fingers that had explored her skin and sent shockwaves of sensuality all over her body.

Like the one coiling right through her at that moment.

A whisper of a five-o'clock shadow darkened his cheeks, giving him a rugged, renegade look, and his chestnut hair looked just tousled enough to make her want to run her fingers through it.

He turned to her, his expression suddenly serious. "Something tells me you're not thinking about your family."

"Nope."

He raked her with a quick glance, then turned back to the road. "About the VoiceBox product-launch party?"

"Nope."

"About an alternative destination for this car."

"Yep."

He grinned. "We're not far from the estate. But you name the place and I'll take you there."

"Home."

"You are totally confusing me, woman."

The way he said *woman* nearly did her in. "I meant your home."

She saw him swallow. "That's another hour south of here."

"Chicken."

A smile danced on those amazing lips. "I've been called worse."

"Like?"

"Gentleman."

"Why is that worse?"

"Because I'm trying like hell to be one. And you—" he flashed her another look, smoky and sincere "—are killing me."

Delight danced through her at the thought. "I'm not doing anything," she responded with mock indignity. "I'm sitting here, listening to music."

"You're eating me up with your eyes and inviting yourself to my house."

She couldn't help laughing. "I am not," she lied. "I'm doing what I always do…weighing the options. Considering both sides of the argument."

He slowed as they reached the iron gate of the main entrance to the estate. "Which side is winning?"

"Ohh." Uncertainty colored her tone. "Kiss or hand-shake? Kiss or handshake? Which shall it be?"

Suddenly he pulled into the main drive and slid his car door up to the security dial pad. All that dancing delight dropped to her stomach with a thud of disappointment.

"Let me decide for you," he said, lowering his window with the press of a button. "I think you should go home, talk to your family, concentrate on work, get a good night's sleep, and when I call you tomorrow, we can arrange a time for our next meeting." He took a deep breath and held his hand out to her. "Go for the handshake, Paige, as you would with any business acquaintance or platonic friend."

She looked at his hand but didn't touch it. "That's a reasonable way to look at the situation."

He dropped the hand he'd offered and cocked his head toward the keypad. "Now, do you want to tell me the secret code, or will you have to kill me afterward?"

Moistening her lips, she slowly unlatched her seat belt, never taking her gaze from his.

With a slow smile she climbed out of her seat, turned carefully and eased herself onto his lap, facing him. She could feel the steering wheel at her back, but focused on his shocked face in front of her. She felt his whole body—every masculine inch—stiffen under her.

"We never tell anyone our code." She held her right hand out the window and touched the keypad without taking her eyes off him.

She punched in the five digits. Slowly.

She could have sworn he stifled a moan.

As the gate rumbled open in front of the car, they both sat motionless. Heat burned where they touched as he hardened and she melted.

Then she leaned toward his mouth, pressing her breasts to his chest, loving how his pewter gaze darkened as his pupils dilated with arousal.

"What are you doing, Paige?" he ground out.

"Just making the other side of that argument," she whispered, her lips almost touching his.

She could feel his heart thundering like hers. They were so close. No more than a breath apart. The needy ache between her legs rippled through her whole body, making her nipples hurt, her fingers twitch, her mouth water.

"You make one hell of a compelling argument, Paige." His voice was tight, as a single vein pulsed under a muscle in his neck. Sending blood, she knew, to one place in his body.

She rolled her bottom ever so slightly against him, as a shot of pure, womanly desire heated her. "It's the curse of a fair-minded person."

"Your fair mind is having quite an effect on me," he said roughly. "And if you don't move, I'm going to go from gentleman to hot-blooded male in about three seconds."

She didn't move a muscle.

"Two."

She closed her eyes.

"One."

She parted her lips.

He whispered her name as he inched closer to kiss her, but she backed up at precisely the same time. Then she extended her hand to him. For a simple, business-like shake.

"Thank you for your company, Mr. Camberlane."

His jaw dropped as he closed his hand over hers.

"Please have your secretary call my office at your earliest convenience so we can…meet again."

With one hand she grabbed her bag, flipped open his door and slid out of the car. Then she turned and walked up the drive without giving him the satisfaction of turning around.

That was balanced, she thought smugly. Not fair, but balanced.

"I feel like I'm going to blow breakfast every time I stand up. It's like I have no control over my own body. Do you know that feeling?"

No control over her body? Yes, Paige knew exactly how Megan felt. But her loss of physical control had nothing to do with pregnancy and everything to do with the restless night of erotic fantasies that had kept her awake.

"We're cool today, Meg," Paige addressed the speaker phone on her desk as she booted up her computer to check the day's calendar. "Did you leave me any major headaches from yesterday?"

"Yesterday was quiet. But tell me more about what happened at Louret."

"I told you." Paige clicked a few keystrokes and opened up her daily calendar. "Caroline and Jillian were very kind and sweet. Oh, and Grant is still staying there."

"Really? Well, he's got a lot of history to sort."

"I think he's more interested in the present than the past."

Megan was quiet for a second, and Paige waited for her to ask what the comment meant. "You there, Meg?"

"Mmm. Just sipping tea. Did you see Jack?"

"Oh, yes. He's unbelievable."

"Is he as cute as his picture?"

Paige decided to focus on his appeal. The uncanny resemblance to their father would be obvious when Megan saw him. "Even more so in real life. He's the sweetest little thing. Called me Pay."

"Awww."

"Yeah, he's adorable." Paige studied the calendar on her screen. "There's only one meeting scheduled with a prospective client this afternoon and two event consultants from Silicon Valley who want to do a dog-and-pony show. I can handle it today."

Before Megan answered, Paige's office door burst open. Her brother Trace stood in the doorway, his face pale and his green eyes dazed.

"Go lie down," Paige told her sister. "I'll check in with you in a few hours."

As soon as she hung up with Megan, Paige stood and came around her desk. "What's the matter, Trace?"

He just shook his head. "I—I just saw someone."

"Who?"

He glanced over his shoulder as though the apparition had followed him into their upstairs offices. "Just…no one. I must have imagined it."

An eerie chill skittered down her spine. "A ghost?"

He just laughed lightly at the obvious implication. "No, Dad's not wandering around the estate with a chain and the Ghost of Christmas Past. Not yet, anyway."

"Then who was it?"

He shook his head. "I just thought I saw someone I knew."

"Who?"

"It was a mistake. Just looked like someone I once knew."

Something in his voice touched Paige. "A lady?" she asked with a teasing smile.

"Not exactly a 'lady,' but definitely a woman."

Intrigued by the uncharacteristic wistfulness in the comment, Paige tried to push him into one of the chairs in front of her desk. "Tell me more."

But his stoic, reserved demeanor had returned as suddenly as it had disappeared. "Not important, Paige. I just came up here to get the rundown on your meeting at The Vines. Why didn't you join us for dinner last night, by the way?"

"I was busy." Fantasizing.

"With Camberlane?" he asked pointedly, his tease not quite as light as hers had been.

"Of course not," she said quickly. "I'd been gone all day. I had to catch up. My visit went very well, I think."

"Eli backing off his threats?"

"I don't know," she admitted. "I don't think he has Caroline's support to overturn the divorce settlement. She appears to be firmly opposed to opening that can of worms. But he and Cole are determined to contest the will. That isn't going to change. They're just waiting for the murder investigation to get closer to a resolution."

Trace folded his arms and stared into the adjacent sunroom that Paige used as a conference area. "I hope to hell they don't have to wait long. I want this thing resolved."

"You and me both," Paige agreed.

Her desk phone beeped, and line one flashed.

"I'll let you get back to work," Trace said with a nod to her phone.

Paige leaned over her desk to read the Caller ID. *Symphonics, Inc. Office of the CEO.*

Why did that make her heart leap and her throat close? "Yeah, this is a client."

As Trace passed her desk, he glanced at the readout. "One of your favorites, too." With a brotherly wink, he left her alone to talk to…her client.

* * *

Matt almost hung up before she answered. Why was he calling her first thing in the morning? Was he that gone over her?

"Paige Ashton."

Just the sound of her voice answered his question. Yep. That gone. "Don't tell me you don't have Caller ID."

Her laugh was easy, quick. "I do."

"And I get the formal hello?"

"The same hello I give all my clients. No different from my...handshake."

Yeah. Her handshake. The one that had him nursing severe masculine discomfort all the way back to Half Moon Bay. The handshake that made him sweat.

"So, how are you this morning?" he asked casually.

"Fine, thank you. And you?"

He was the one who said they should keep it businesslike. It was all part of the battle of the brain and the body, and he'd won round one. Barely.

"I'd like to schedule that tour, and a meeting to go over some of the event details," he said, purposely formal.

"Of course. How's Friday morning?"

"How's Saturday night?" Screw formality.

For a moment she said nothing. He heard a keyboard click. Was she checking her calendar or deliberately making him wait?

"Let's compromise, Matt." Her voice was silky smooth. Like every other inch of her.

Oh, boy. Round two would be tough.

"I can compromise," he agreed.

"Let's make it Friday afternoon. And if we, uh, run into Friday night, then we'll take it from there."

He smiled into the phone. "It's a date."

"No. It's a meeting."

"Of course," he said with a laugh. "That's what I meant."

When he hung up, Matt strode over to the window of his office, looking out at the koi pond where a group of software engineers sat around a stone table, a laptop open, a few taking notes, one standing to make an emphatic point.

*That* was a meeting, he thought.

What he had in mind with Paige was...he closed his eyes and remembered the feel of her body as she spread her legs over his lap.

Shaking his head, he turned back to his desk. For one insane moment he considered calling Auberge to make reservations for the weekend.

But then he remembered those tears. And his promise to Walker. So, platonic and businesslike it had to be. He could do that, he repeated for the gajillionth time. Couldn't he?

But maybe he should call that hotel in Napa just in case he lost round two.

# Eight

**M**att pushed his luck by arriving at four-thirty on Friday afternoon. It was technically still afternoon. But perilously close to evening. To dinnertime.

Paige breezed into the event-planning reception area the minute he arrived.

"We're too late to take a tour of the winery," she announced, a hint of accusation in her voice.

He gave her a half smile and made a show of extending his hand. "Hello, Paige."

She gave him a remarkably *un*remarkable handshake. He got the message: this is business, buddy.

"Why don't you come into my office and I can show you the new layout and seating arrangements we've developed?"

He nodded, following her through a single door and short hallway to a spacious office, past her desk, through a set of French doors to a long, narrow solarium. He barely glanced at the mind-boggling vista of autumn vineyards out the wall of windows; his attention was seized by the conference table covered with sketches.

She indicated the papers with a sweep of her hand. "You can take a look at these while I get the creative concepts for the invitations. As soon as you select a design, we'll get them into production. They need to be printed and ready for hand addressing by the end of next week."

She rushed by him, back into the office, but kept talking over her shoulder.

"We've hired a special sound man, and he's arranged with your technical folks to have the VoiceBox software loaded into his system. He'll be programming songs so that every laptop on every table will have the software on it," she said from her office, gathering papers at her desk. "When we do the seating, we'll match up music with the guests. So it's important, when people RSVP, that they tell us ahead of time who they plan to dress as, so we can have music by that artist."

Arms crossed, he leaned into the doorway to observe her, unable to wipe the amused look from his face. She was a whirling dervish, zinging facts and information and moving at the speed of sound. Was that nerves?

From his vantage point, he could see her reach way over her desk to get something. His gaze traveled over her trim form, dressed today in gray slacks and a simple black sweater. The pants were just fitted enough to show the outline of her feminine little derriere, and the sweater was just fuzzy enough to make him want to…pet it.

She straightened and he withdrew from the doorway before she caught him staring.

"I've also met with the chef, and I've worked out three different menu options with wine recommendations, of course," she said, sailing back into the room and filling any empty table space with more papers.

She glanced at her watch. "Some sketches of centerpieces were due here by three, but the courier must be late. You're going to love what we came up with for Madonna."

"A bustier?"

She snapped her finger. "That reminds me. I wanted to go over a list of speakers with you. Will you be making a formal address?"

"A bustier reminded you of me making a speech?" He couldn't resist a teasing grin and a gentle tug at the sleeve of her fluffy sweater. "Slow down, will you?"

"Time is money, they taught us in B-school."

He pulled out a chair and dropped into it with mock exhaustion. "When you work, you make my head spin, you know that?"

She gave him a saucy smile. "You should see when I play."

Desire sucker punched him at the thought.

"Plus," she narrowed her blue-green eyes at him in accusation, "You are woefully late. We'll never get through all this today."

"All what?"

She pointed at the table. "All this."

He looked at his watch. "It's only four-thirty. You have a date?"

That made her smile.

"Tell you what," he said, pulling out the chair next to him. "You sit down, take me through every imaginable detail, then we'll go out to dinner and discuss anything we can't cover here."

"Okay," she finally said, taking the seat. "But I'm serious, Matt, we've got a lot to cover if we're going to pull off this party."

He nodded in agreement and scooted his chair closer to her. "I'm all yours."

"Yeah, right," she mumbled, pulling the sketches closer. "Let's start with the room layout."

Paige moved through her agenda with speed and efficiency. She had done an impressive job of preparation, offering him two or three creative options for every element of the party and checking off a master list every time he made a decision.

He'd been so wrapped up in fighting the physical attraction, he'd forgotten how damn bright she was, how focused. He liked the way she concentrated on each issue. He liked the way she presented every idea. He liked the way she argued and analyzed and…smelled. Hell, he *loved* the way she smelled.

Inching just a little closer, they examined various invitation concepts, their heads practically touching as they rearranged table placements, finalized the invitation list and reviewed the menu.

"I'm not so sure about the autumn duck salad," she said, gnawing a little on her bottom lip.

"Why not?" He was far more interested in the taste of that lip than the duck salad.

"Because I really think you want a marinated duck breast with butternut squash."

What he wanted was to kiss that mouth. "I do." He caught himself. "I do?"

"Mmm." Her eyelids closed with a sensual moan that left him slack-jawed as he watched. "The duck breast is to die for with our sparkling Pinot Noir. Just unimaginably delicious."

Speaking of delicious... His gaze was riveted to her mouth. Then it dropped to her throat. And landed at the little V-neck of the black sweater.

"Matt," she said softly.

"Yeah?"

"I'm losin' you, buddy."

He laughed and snagged her gaze. "Quite the contrary. But this talk of marinades and..." *breasts* "duck is getting me hungry."

He was perilously close to kissing her. One inch, two and their lips would meet. The air literally hummed between them.

"Paige? Are you in here?" A voice called from Paige's office.

Paige jerked her chair back, but not quickly enough.

A woman stood in the doorway grinning broadly. "Oh, I didn't realize you were with a *client.*"

He stood immediately, recognizing Megan Ashton and the implication in her voice. He doubted Paige got quite that close to most clients.

She stood also, smoothing her slacks and stepping a good two feet away from him. "You've met Matt Camberlane, Meg. Matt, my sister Megan Pearce."

Megan gave him a firm handshake and held his gaze with her brilliant green eyes. "It's nice to see you again, Matt." She looked beyond him at the ocean of paper they'd created on the conference room table. Her lips curled in a teasing smile. "So, are you two making any progress? On the event, I mean."

He laughed, liking her wit immediately. "Are you kidding? She's a slave driver. Can't even get her to quit for dinner."

Megan raised one brow and glanced at her sister. "I'm sure you can talk her into a quick bite somewhere."

The sisters shared a look, making Matt wonder just how much Paige had confided.

"As a matter of fact, we were just closing up here," he said. As much as he hated to, he knew the right thing to do in this situation. "Would you care to join us for dinner in town?"

Her eyes widened along with her smile. "Thank you, Matt. But the VoiceBox event is all Paige's, and I'm sure you two have many, uh, details to discuss."

Paige cleared her throat and put a hand on her hip. "Did you come in here just to throw around innuendos, Meg, or are you saying goodbye for the weekend?"

Megan laughed lightly and put an affectionate hand on Paige's shoulder. "Both, if you must know the truth. But not for the weekend. I'm coming back tomorrow morning. We're having a...family gathering."

"Really?" Paige frowned. "First I've heard of it."

"Evidently the detectives want to review some evidence with all of us and go over the progress of the investigation."

"On a Saturday?"

"It's the only time Walker could fly in. He'll be here tomorrow morning. The meeting's at eleven."

Paige nodded in understanding. "Okay. I hope they've made some progress."

"We all do." Megan turned to the door and caught Matt's eye. "Great to see you again, Matt. I hope you are thrilled with the Ashton event-planning services."

"I'm crazy about her—er, them."

Megan just laughed on her way out.

They agreed on everything, even the fact that the unseasonably warm evening called for beer, not wine. Tucked into a corner booth at Downtown Joes, one of the most unpretentious restaurants in Napa Valley, Paige and Matt sipped something the microbrewery called Tail Waggin' Amber Ale and listened to the buzz of the locals and the strains of Bruce Springsteen in the background.

Paige's slender fingers curled around the frosty mug and Matt debated the desire to reach over and take her hand. How could something that felt so right be such a battle?

Instead he drummed his fingers over the ever-present imaginary keyboard on the table.

"Where did you learn to play the piano?" she asked.

"Self-taught."

"Really? No lessons?"

He almost laughed. As if they could have afforded lessons. "No, no lessons. No piano in my house." Or apartment. Or trailer. Or wherever Dianne Camberlane was waitressing when he was a child.

"So how did you learn?"

"The first piano I ever played was in a bar. Not like this one—" he looked around with a rueful glance "—a little more downscale."

"Where was that?"

He took a sip of ale to buy a moment of time and decide how much to reveal. "My mom worked the closing shift one summer when I was eleven or so. She didn't have a sitter, so I used to hang out while she worked."

"In a bar?" Her eyes, which looked remarkably blue in the dim light of the restaurant, widened.

And not just any bar, he thought wryly. The Dragon Lady in Modesto was in a league of lowlife all its own.

He shrugged. "Yeah, in a bar. But there was this piano, and I started to pluck out songs."

"By ear?"

"I have a good ear for music. Then I found some sheet music in the piano bench. Old and yellowed, and left over from the fifties, when," he laughed again, "that piano was last tuned."

She smiled and ran a finger around the rim of her glass. "Don't tell me. Frank Sinatra songs."

"You got it, sweetheart." He grinned and hummed the opening notes of "Fly Me to the Moon" as he "played" the table. "I knew those songs because my grandmother, believe it or not, used to play records of Frankie when I would visit her. I guess I was always a bit of a techno nerd. I just started to sight-read music."

"That's not nerdy. That's genius."

"Hardly, but there is a close association between math and music. They both come naturally to me. I don't use any of the right fingering. I tried to take formal lessons in college, but didn't learn much except what all the Italian words mean."

"What Italian words?"

*"Fortissimo. Diminuendo. Pianissimo."*

She gave him a questioning look.

"Very loud, gradually softer and very soft. The little italic instructions you see on sheet music. Until I took a lesson, I just played that stuff from feel."

"From feel." She folded her arms over the table. "You are a very sensual man, aren't you?"

Here we go. Round two about to start. "I like music." He couldn't resist leaning closer and lowering his voice. "Does that make me sensual?"

"You do everything like that—from *feel*." Her gaze dropped over his face, lingered on his mouth and returned to his eyes.

"I trust my gut instinct, if that's what you mean." And

his gut was screaming to close the space and devour her with one long Tail Waggin' Amber Ale kiss. "That's how I learned music. And how I got through college and the Army and how I built my business."

"Is that how you got through your divorce?"

He inched back, more from the edge in her tone than the fact that they'd never discussed that he'd been married. "I guess if I had trusted my gut instinct on that one, I never would have gotten married."

"So what happened?" There was that focus he'd admired so much in her office. But this time it was directed at him, so it was even more impressive. Or terrifying, depending on your point of view.

"It was a mistake."

"How so?"

"Brooke, that was my…" God, he hated calling her his wife. He studied the condensation around his mug. "She was an acquirer of goods, my ex-wife. World class. And once I had my mug on the cover of *Fortune Magazine,* she decided I was the must-have accessory that season."

"You seem too smart to get snagged by a gold digger."

"Oh, no." He shook his head. "Brooke wasn't digging for gold. She had plenty of her own, thanks to her family. She was just looking for—I don't know. A conquest. The ultimate catch." The beer coagulated in his stomach as he thought about how he'd been used.

"What were *you* looking for?"

His throat suddenly dry, despite the ale, he managed a rough laugh. "Easy, sweetheart. You've already extracted more personal information from me than any woman in years, and now you want divorce details?"

She just looked at him, her eyes shifting hues as quickly as the topics. Whatever the color, they were inviting. Intimate. Way, way too intimate. "Yes. I want details. What were you looking for when you got married?"

Good God, would that waiter never come?

He pulled off a totally casual shrug. "What any guy who hangs around an altar in a tux and makes promises wants. A lifetime of contentment and happiness. Right?"

She nodded slowly, still regarding him with…distrust? Skepticism? Well-founded skepticism, he should tell her. Oh, what the hell. "Unfortunately," he admitted, "I married someone who didn't think those promises—you know, love, honor and cherish—included anything as mundane as monogamy."

She sank into the seat a little and frowned in empathy.

"But I'm sure I was as much to blame—"

"That's not true!" She interrupted him. "It's not your fault if your wife was unfaithful."

He held up a hand to stop her sweet defense. "I married her for the wrong reasons, too. I thought her social status gave me a credibility that my, uh, upbringing didn't afford."

She closed her eyes for a moment, but when she looked back, all that skepticism was gone. "You know, Matt, my parents' marriage was really no different. My mother, the former secretary, married my father for social credibility. And my father—" she shook her head "—he didn't know the meaning of the word *monogamy*."

"I know that," he said quietly. "That's always dismayed Walker, too. That's why I have no doubt about his commitment to Tamra. And—" he exhaled slowly and almost reached for her hand "—that's why I bet you'll make someone a loyal, loving wife." Someone? Yeah, some real lucky bastard.

She leaned all the way back in the booth and squinted

at him. "So since your marriage, you've never considered getting involved with anyone else?"

Wasn't round two supposed to be about sex? How the hell did she drag him into this discussion? "Depends on your definition of *involved*," he said with a suggestive grin. "I am a healthy thirty-year-old man with a normal appetite."

"I'm healthy, too." Her look was equally suggestive. Downright provocative, in fact. "And so is my, uh, appetite."

His pulse accelerated, shooting a couple of gallons of blood southward. "Your appetite?" he managed to ask.

The waiter appeared with a tray overflowing with burgers and fries.

"Perfect timing," Matt said, hoping his relief wasn't too evident. "The lady just said she's got quite an appetite."


"Do you have to drive all the way back to Half Moon Bay tonight?" Paige asked as he pulled into the slow Friday-night Napa traffic.

"No, I took that suite at Auberge again." He glanced at her, everything in him wanting to ask her to come there with him. But that would only lead to a devastating loss of round two.

After their dinner had arrived, they'd managed to stay out of dangerous territory and avoid any more personal revelations.

Without warning she laid a light hand on his thigh. Through the fabric he could feel the warmth of her touch. "Want to take a drive?" she suggested.

"Sure." He turned right on Trancas, out of the clogged traffic.

"The Silverado Trail?" she asked. "Doesn't that go straight to Auberge?"

But they were not going to his hotel, he vowed silently. Because if he had her anywhere near a bedroom, he could kiss his willpower goodbye. "We'll just go up to the river reserve. It's a pretty night."

He glanced up at the waxing moon, the clear sky and about a hundred stars. Romance. That was okay. Some stars, moon and evening air. He had a blanket in the trunk, wrapped around some old albums he was taking into a record exchange the next day.

They meandered through a winding road, surrounded on both sides by the recently harvested Chardonnay vineyards, then hit the crossroad that linked the trail to Route 29.

"You know your way around Napa," she commented.

"I like it up here," he said vaguely. "I think I'll retire in Napa."

"Retire? You're thirty."

He could afford to retire that minute, but he still had too much to do with Symphonics. "Eventually. When I hit the big five-oh."

"And won't that be fun," she said with a hint of wry bitterness in her voice, "just you and…your piano?"

He got the message. And it stung. Yep. Just him and his piano. And Paige would no doubt be raising children and doing volunteer work and making that lucky bastard the happiest guy on earth.

"There's the entrance to the reserve," she commented as he drove past it. "Maybe you don't know your way around here all that well after all."

No. He'd just been mentally lost for a moment.

What was he doing? Bringing her here to make out

on the grass? Tease her with promises of romance…to what end?

"This isn't a good idea," he said, his voice tight.

She didn't respond.

With one swift movement, he turned the car and headed back down the Silverado Trail, toward her home.

From the moment he'd shown up in her office, Paige's whole body had purred with electricity and pulsed with expectation. But it just thunked into reality with one unexpected U-turn.

He didn't want her.

He wanted sex; he was, after all, "a healthy thirty-year-old man." But his sudden change of heart and the way he zipped that little sports car toward the Ashton Estate told her one thing.

He didn't want her.

Only, that contradicted everything his eyes and hands and mouth and body language had been screaming since…well, since they'd met.

When they reached the edge of the reflecting pool in the estate driveway, he turned off the engine and opened his door.

An ache that had nothing to do with desire closed her throat. She put a hand on his arm before he got out of the car.

"Matt, wait. What's going on?"

His eyes were stormy gray and sent a clear message of frustration, but he didn't say anything.

"We've got ourselves in quite a spot, don't we?" she asked gently. "I'd rather not end the evening on this uncomfortable note."

He smiled wistfully. "You're a natural peacemaker, aren't you, Paige? You like everything to be…nice."

"I don't know about that," she said. "I do like everyone to be happy."

"Are you?"

"Are *you*?" she countered.

He leaned back into his seat and raked a hand through his hair, leaving it endearingly messy. "Hell, no."

"What's the matter?"

He turned to her. "You're way too smart not to know the answer to that."

She swallowed hard and decided to stop any kind of games. She wanted him. She didn't want to fight that anymore. "I would have gone back to your hotel," she said simply. "I wanted to."

He closed his eyes. "I know that."

"Then what's the matter?"

He slid a hand under her jaw, cupping her chin and easing her face toward him. "I tried to tell you this the first time I kissed you. The first time we…almost…"

"What, Matt? Tell me what?"

"You deserve better than 'sex without strings.'"

She closed her eyes. "Maybe I do, Matt. But right now, tonight, with you, I don't care about the strings. I want you."

His mouth came over hers instantly, his lips warm and open and delicious. Like a struck match, the fire flared in her, and she wrapped her arms around his neck and pulled him closer.

Their tongues fused and curled around each other as her heart walloped against her rib cage. Oh, how she wanted this. She wanted his hands and his mouth and his body all over her.

She leaned into him, lifting her chest in a silent invitation for his touch. His hand stroked her sleeve, and his fingers tightened his grip as though he were forcing himself not to touch where they both wanted him to touch.

He pulled away, his breath already tight and quick. "Let me walk you to the door." He got out of the car before she could respond.

Why was he fighting her so damn hard?

When he opened her door, she looked up at him, the moonlight carving shadows on his handsome face. He eased her up, then placed a gentle kiss on her head.

"I told you what I want," she whispered. "What do you want?"

He responded with another soul-wrenching kiss, pulling her against his hard, male body, pressing their chests and hips and legs together. She wrapped her arms around his powerful shoulders and clung to him because her knees were shaking and her whole lower half was literally melting.

"What I want," he said gruffly, dropping his face into her hair and letting out an exasperated sigh. "I can't have what I want."

She backed away enough to see his face. "Can't, Matt? I thought you—"

He touched her lips to quiet her. "I *won't*, then. And I do know the difference between the two."

Dropping his mouth against her hair, he slid his hands over her back and waist, then eased her away from him. "Goodnight, Paige."

As she stood in her doorway and watched the lights of the Ferrari disappear down the driveway, she made an easy decision, unencumbered by a single second of self-doubt or debate.

Maybe he "won't"… but she would. Oh, yes, she would. Right now.

# Nine

**M**att stood on the balcony of his suite and stared at the moonlit hills of the Napa Valley. He took a long swig of the beer he'd grabbed out of the minibar and closed his eyes as the ice-cold liquid slid down his throat.

He'd finish this beer, take a shower—just as cold— and go to bed. Or, he might stand on this deck, gaze at stars and congratulate himself for winning round two for the next few hours. 'Cause he sure as hell wasn't going to sleep.

What was it about that girl that got him going so much? Sure she was pretty. Not beautiful, not even as striking as her sister, Megan. But beguiling, somehow, delicate and feminine and natural. Of course, she was sexy. Not vixenlike, but her sensuality was subtle, like her woman's body. Not in your face, and even more appealing because of it.

But there was something else about Paige. That quiet

intelligence. That secret twinkle in her eye. The honesty of her smile.

Plus she kissed like—oh. He blew out a long, slow breath as arousal tightened its familiar grip on his lower half. Might be time for that icy shower.

The only explanation that made sense is that he wanted her because he couldn't have her. Why couldn't he have her?

Oh, yeah. Because he'd promised Walker he wouldn't hurt her. And because she was too valuable a gem to end up on his ever-growing discard pile. And mostly because, once he had sex with her, this attraction that had taken hold of his brain and body would disappear and then he'd have to have The Conversation:

"I know you're looking for something more serious…"

"Look, I'm married to my job and just not interested in a commitment…"

"You're a great girl and I know you want someone you can count on…"

"I'm not looking for a long-term relationship…"

Hell, he'd used every line in the book and probably made up a few new ones in the process. God, he hated The Conversation. And the thought of having it with Paige…

The beer suddenly lost its taste as the moon slid behind a cloud, leaving Matt with the sickening self-disgust of a man who really didn't want to look in the mirror the next day.

But why should he be disgusted? He'd done it. He'd walked away and won round two. He'd conquered the body with the brain. He hadn't given in to that sweet, impossible ache she caused in him. He hadn't succumbed to that overwhelming need to *have* her. Hadn't surrendered to that desire to—

He froze at the tentative knock on the door.

He distinctly remembered placing the Do Not Disturb While I Congratulate Myself for Being a Hero sign on the door. Not like the customer-pleasing Auberge du Soleil staff to ignore that.

He walked slowly into the living room, the first few measures of an unholy anticipation beginning a foxtrot through his veins.

Who would knock on his suite at eleven o'clock at night?

The second rap was far less tentative.

Who knew he was staying at the Auberge that night?

"Matt?"

Oh, God. So much for heroics.

He flipped the lock and opened the door, his throat tight and his heart fully engaged in a drum solo now. He just stared at her, literally speechless.

"I suspected you might be a creature of habit," Paige said with that honest smile he'd just been thinking about. "I figured you'd stay in the same room. So I took a chance."

She took a chance? That was the understatement of the century.

Her gaze darted over his shoulder. "You are alone, aren't you?"

He choked a quick laugh and opened the door wider, his brain cells making a futile attempt at something that might resemble the English language. He wanted to ask what she was doing there, but that would have been a rhetorical question. If he could have formed the question at all.

*Paige Ashton had followed him back to his suite.*

Somehow, his overworked gray matter just couldn't get past that.

She still wore the black sweater and gray pants, but the look on her face was different. It was a look of a woman who...

"Do you have another one of those?"

He followed her gaze down to the beer bottle he still held.

"Never mind," she said, strolling past by him and dropping her handbag on the chaise. The chaise where he'd half undressed her not so long ago. "I'll just have some ice water."

He stared at her.

"Unless you'd rather I get it myself while you figure out some easy way to close your jaw."

That made him laugh. "I wasn't expecting you." Speaking of stupid understatements. "What are you—" And stupid questions. "*Why* are you here?"

Her eyes flashed. Green, now. A nice, inviting shade of sage, he noticed. "If you have to ask, Matt, maybe I'd better turn around and go home."

"No, don't do that," he said quickly. "I'll get you some water."

While he did, she stepped through the sliding doors to the balcony. He opened a plastic water bottle and poured it into a hotel glass, then freed some ice from a miniature tray he found in the freezer. Did she have to have ice?

Yes. She had to cool off.

Because the look in those green eyes was anything but cool.

He joined her on the balcony, the ice clanging pleasantly in the glass as he handed it to her. As though it was perfectly normal for Paige Ashton to show up in his hotel room and share a cold drink in the moonlight.

She took a long, slow sip, her eyes closed, her throat moving with each swallow.

"I was just thinking about you," he admitted as she finished.

Her eyes opened slowly and locked on his. "What were you thinking?"

He couldn't help grinning. He was so damn glad to see her. "I'm going to venture a guess that I was thinking the same thing you were thinking when you got in your car, threw caution to the wind and knocked on a door you weren't entirely sure was mine."

"Yeah. We're definitely on the same wavelength here."

She put the glass on a cocktail table and leaned back, placing her hands on the railing behind her. A stance, he couldn't help noticing, that was clear in its non-verbal communication. No crossed arms. No barriers. Absolutely no second thoughts.

Who knew Paige was such a woman of…action?

"Would you like to know what I'm thinking now, Matt?"

He took a step closer and put his hands on top of hers, effectively pinning her to the railing. "Let me guess."

She tilted her face toward him, her lips parted.

"You're thinking that this physical attraction is just too powerful to resist."

Her eyes twinkled in agreement.

"And you're thinking, what's the harm? He's single, I'm single, we like each other and life's short. Why not just give in to the lust?"

Her lips tipped up as she gave him an imperceptible nod.

"And," he continued, "you're obviously thinking you have to make the first move or—in this case—the second move since we've already been in this suite once before…." He dipped closer to that pretty mouth. "You figure I won't, because I'm a gentleman and a client and your cousin's good friend."

Her eyes darkened at that. "You were right until that point. I guarantee you I am not thinking about Walker right now."

Then maybe he should stop thinking about Walker, too.

"I promised him," Matt said slowly. "That I wouldn't hurt you."

She glided her hands up and down his arms. "For one thing, I don't answer to Walker. And for another," she locked her hands behind his neck, forcing him even closer. "This isn't going to hurt."

She lifted herself up and kissed him. Gently at first, easily. Lips closed, eyes open.

"See? Did that hurt?"

He bit back a low groan. "Define *hurt*."

She leaned into him, her taut breasts pressing the fabric of his shirt. The kiss that accompanied that move included a tiny taste of tongue.

"I'm a grown woman, Matt," she whispered.

He ran his hands over the tight muscles of her back and let them settle in the little dip just above her backside. "I definitely noticed that."

"I won't break," she promised.

She pulled him in for a kiss so deep it silenced all the voices in his head. Even the sound of The Conversation he'd eventually have to have.

She'd come to him, she knew what she was doing and he…he couldn't fight this. He couldn't fight her sweet woman's body or her sensual, daring kisses.

She'd started round three—and he didn't have a prayer.

She dropped her head back and offered him her throat, which he covered with heated kisses in a trail down the V-neck of her sweater.

His hands glided over the feather-soft cashmere, over her shoulder, over her breast, where he paused to caress the feminine swell. Her breath caught in her throat, and he froze.

"Paige." He could feel her nipple harden. He grazed his fingertips over the bud, his mouth literally watering to suckle her. "Honey, are you sure?"

Her eyes widened and her expression shifted from one of wanton arousal to dead serious. "Matt, I won't cry," she promised quietly. "I swear I won't." She took his hand off her breast and laced her fingers through his, pulling their joined fist to her lips and pressing a kiss on his flesh. "I know what I'm doing. I want to make love to you."

·   His heart squeezed at the words.

He wanted to have sex. She wanted to make love.

But before he could clarify the semantics, she took his hand and guided it under her sweater. He sucked in a sharp breath as he realized she had nothing on underneath.

Had she been braless all night? During their meeting? During dinner? A blast of heat shot through him at the thought, making him rock hard. His fingers explored her tender skin, and she leaned farther back as he tugged the sweater higher and exposed her breasts.

Sex or love or whatever. He'd lost this round when he opened the door.

"Beautiful," he muttered as he looked at her. He cupped a hand under her chin and lifted her face. "You are beautiful, Paige Ashton, you know that?"

She straightened and reached down to the bottom of

her sweater. In one move, she had it over her head and flung it on a chair. "You make me feel that way."

His whole being clutched in need. Wordlessly he spun her around in his arms, pulling her warm back to his chest. Wrapping her in his arms, his kissed her silky shoulders and caressed her bare breasts with hungry hands.

As he led her toward the darkened bedroom, he could almost swear he heard the final bell. *"Ladies and gentlemen, the body has won. The brain is down for the count."*

As they passed the bathroom, he reached into his toiletry kit that lay open on the counter. Grabbing three condoms, he continued to walk her toward the bed that had been thoughtfully turned down by the efficient Auberge staff.

Easing her onto the sheets, he traced the gentle curves of her body, delving his tongue deep into her mouth with every kiss. Leaning up to take his shirt off, he blinked, adjusting to the dim light. She studied him openly, stroking his chest as though she were memorizing every muscle, her lips parted as short, quick breaths escaped.

Then she reached up and touched his lower lip with one finger, sending a lightning bolt right down to his already painful erection. "Speaking of what's been on our minds—" she slipped her finger into his mouth and back out again "—I've been thinking about this a lot," she whispered.

"Yeah," he laughed softly. "Me, too."

"So it's your turn. What do you think about, when you think about me?"

He leaned over her and very, very softly kissed her lips. "I think about how sweet you are, how smart and funny and good at your job."

She let out a low, slow laugh of disbelief. "Yeah," she mocked him. "Me, too."

He laughed with her. "Okay. I also, occasionally, when I'm absolutely unable to stop myself, I consider…this." He bent over her breast and circled the nipple with his tongue. Slowly at first, then faster as the bud swelled and she began to moan.

"Then," he continued, as he transferred his attention to her other breast, "I amuse myself by imagining this."

Kissing a trail down her stomach, he easily unfastened her slacks and slid them over her hips, revealing surprisingly sexy black lace underwear. Man, the girl was full of surprises tonight.

When she'd kicked the slacks off, he placed his hands low on her hip bones so that his thumbs practically touched, right above the soft rise of her mound.

"And I have been known," he said in low voice, "to ponder the possibilities of doing this." He dipped his tongue into the top of the panties.

Her fingers dug into his hair as he slid the whisper of silk over her legs.

"Yep," she laughed softly. "Great minds really do think alike."

His eyes had finally adjusted to the dark, and he could see the soft damp curls between her legs, and the rapid rise and fall of her stomach with each tight breath.

"And this is a particular favorite fantasy of mine." His voice was strained with the need to taste her. He started to bend her knees, so he could explore her slick mound with his tongue, but instead she slipped her hand under his arm and pulled him up for another deep kiss. Then he unfastened his trousers and she helped him finish undressing.

Wrapping her legs around him, she reached between

them, and grasped him. "I can't wait," she whispered. "Put the condom on."

As soon as he did, she arched and guided him straight into her. He gasped at the sudden heat, at the snug enclosure, and at her uncharacteristic boldness.

Although, he was beginning to discover, maybe it wasn't so uncharacteristic after all.

He rasped her name in surprise and shifted his weight on top of her, plunging deeper as she lifted her hips, shocking himself with the intense pleasure.

Their rhythm started slowly, then built like a piece of classical music. A steady, rolling melody, then a fast, anxious staccato, and finally, a crescendo. He buried his face into the sweet, damp flesh of her neck, inhaling the scent of their bodies and heat as he pumped into the tight, hot envelope of her body and fought the last of his fight.

Her nails dug into his flesh and her lashes fluttered as her control slipped away. Along with his.

Her flesh tightened around him as she arched higher and faster, every breath more strained than the one before.

He sounded just as ragged, just as far gone.

He'd lost his battle, lost his sense, lost his control. He'd *lost,* plain and simple.

As he plummeted over the edge and emptied everything he had into her, his brain managed one brief, coherent and completely unfamiliar thought.

Winning was overrated.


"What did you wish for?"

Matt's question, the first sound Paige heard before opening her eyes, was so soft and so low that a shiver ran over her whole body at the sensation.

For a moment she couldn't process the question. Instead she inhaled the warm aroma of his chest, where her face rested. Her legs were ribboned around his muscular thighs, a coarse dusting of male body hair tickling her flesh. His arm was locked around her, and one of his hands had found a permanent home on top of her breast.

A powerful morning erection prodded her hip, making her realize if she just swiveled an inch, he could slide right back into her. Again.

"Moot point," she murmured. "My wish came true last night."

He chuckled softly. "You wished to sleep with me?"

Lifting her head from its warm, safe haven, she opened her eyes and caught the glint in his wolf-gray gaze. "I'm not that greedy, Matt. I just wished you would kiss me."

"You did?" He seemed genuinely surprised.

"And since you kissed me a hundred times in the last six hours, I got my wish."

His hand caressed her breast, his strong, long fingers easily palming her whole rib cage. She made that one inch swivel and his velvety manhood slid between her legs.

She tilted her face toward his and they kissed again.

"One hundred and one," they said in unison, which made them both laugh.

"But you didn't say where I should kiss you." He slid his hand down her stomach, and dipped a finger into her. She was tender from multiple sessions of lovemaking during the night, but the fiery response was instant. Her laugh melted into a sigh of pleasure.

"I only had a penny." She rocked into him as he slid a second finger into her. "I think that kiss costs a quarter."

Laughing softly, he began a leisurely tour of her body, kissing and suckling while he stoked the fire between her legs. Oh, he was definitely a skilled musician. She started to tell him that, but his mouth had suddenly replaced his fingers and her mind went blank.

Oh, yes. Now this—this was a wish come true. Closing her eyes and stabbing her fingers through his hair, she rose to meet his lips and tongue. He drove his tongue into her, circling her sweet spot, then sucking it with a tender love bite.

As she shuddered, he increased the pressure and held her hips in an unyielding grip, torturing and teasing her until she quaked with a sweet and piercing orgasm.

"I told you to be careful what you wish for," he whispered after he'd kissed his way back up to her face.

She almost laughed, but her body was so heavy from satisfaction, the effort was too much. "You never told me what you wished for," she managed to say, turning her head on the pillow to face him with a sly smile. "Because I'll be happy to make your wishes come true as soon as I can breathe normally again."

For a moment his eyes clouded and the whisper of a frown creased his forehead. Then he lifted his head and looked toward the nightstand. "It's almost nine o'clock. Can you make a family meeting in two hours?"

Her heart sank. "Are you that anxious to get rid of me?"

After a beat, he exhaled and pulled her against him, his arousal obvious. "Does this feel like I'm anxious to get rid of you?"

She slid one leg over his hips and let the male hardness of him settle against her. "You still haven't told me what you wished for."

Surprising her, he tipped her chin up to his face and

kissed her lightly on the nose. "I wished that your cousin wouldn't kill me for seducing you. And if you want to help, you'd better get home with a damn good explanation of where you've been."

She wasn't completely satisfied with that. The whole conversation had an evasive feel about it, but she buried the nagging sensation and started to slide away. "You didn't seduce me," she murmured as they separated.

He grabbed her arm and held her in place. "Paige."

"You're right. I need to get home."

His gaze lingered over her bare body, and she could have sworn he looked…torn? Mad? Scared? "I want to see you again."

"We should have a follow-up meeting next week on the—"

"Not a meeting." His grip tightened ever so slightly. "Just…more of this."

Why did her heart sink at that? She'd made it absolutely clear that she wanted sex. He made it absolutely clear that he was a red-blooded male who wanted the same thing.

Why did "more of this" disappoint her? It was great sex, no strings.

"Can you come to my house?" he asked. "Tonight? I'll make you dinner."

The implied message was as clear as if he'd said "and we can have each other for dessert."

"I don't know," she said vaguely, thrashing around in her brain for a good way to play hard to get. Which wasn't easy when you were naked in bed with a man. "Why don't I call you later and let you know how the meeting goes at home?"

"Why don't you just plan on being at my house at

six o'clock and…" he grazed her thigh with his finger-tip "—plan to spend the night."

Paige waited for that intelligent, rational and usually forceful voice that helped her weigh a decision. The one that kept her levelheaded and balanced. The voice of reason.

But she couldn't hear a thing.

"Okay," she whispered. "I'll be there."

"Coming in the servant's entrance is the oldest trick in the book."

Paige froze at the bottom step of the back entrance and swallowed a curse. Damn. Walker was in the kitchen. She'd purposely driven around to the back of the house to slip in unnoticed and change before the meeting.

"Good morning," she called as she dashed to the back steps that would take her safely to her room upstairs. "Is everybody meeting in the library?"

Without answering, he appeared in the doorway, his piercing dark eyes holding Paige in place as effectively as if he'd reached out with one powerful arm and stopped her.

"Where the hell have you been?"

"Out," she said, lifting her chin and reminding herself that Walker was not her father or her keeper and that she was twenty-two years old and had a master's in business, for crying out loud.

"All night? With Camberlane?"

Why lie? It was a complete waste of time, and Paige didn't believe in lying, anyway. It was the single most-hated trait of her father's. "Yes. All night. With Matt." She sighed and made a feeble attempt to pass him, but all the air seemed to be sucked out of the hallway as Walker created a human wall between her and the stairs.

"Dammit, Paige, how could you be so stupid?"

Anger and frustration coiled through her but she just balled her fists and held her ground. "I don't need you to pass judgment on what's stupid, Walker."

"You are in way over your head with Matt Camberlane."

An image of their lovemaking flashed in her brain. "Thank you for your concern." She made another attempt to pass him and start up the stairs but he refused to move.

"He's a player."

"So I've heard."

"No, I'm telling you, Paige." Walker shook his head and crossed his arms like the commanding Native American he was. "He goes through women like water."

*Plan on spending the night.*

"I'll take my chances," she said with a calm she wasn't exactly sure she felt. "I'm having fun. We like each other. What's the crime in that, Walker?"

"Paige, listen to me." Her cousin's eyes softened, the way they always did when he delivered brotherly advice. Advice she usually wanted and heeded. "He's not ever going to get involved beyond the bedroom. Not with you or anyone."

Her chest tightened, but she refused to let Walker see any reaction. "I know that. He's been perfectly honest with me."

"Maybe he has, but—" Walker shook his head again "—honey, you're not his type. Believe me."

She sure felt like his type last night. "Hey, he bid on me, didn't he?" She tried for a lighthearted voice. "He must have seen something he liked."

"He has a soft spot, too."

Paige scowled at him. "What is that supposed to mean?"

"He felt sorry for you at the auction because you were so uncomfortable." At her look, he continued with a rapid offense. "I was with him, Paige. He bid on you because you were squirming under the lights."

"He paid ten thousand dollars," she said. Her voice sounded weak even to her.

Walker nodded and put a patronizing hand on her shoulder, which she wanted to shake off but suddenly didn't have the fire left in her. "He knew it was for a good cause. And you were looking miserable under those lights."

Miserable? Had she looked miserable to Matt? "Well, we're working together now and—"

"He said 'I'm not interested in her,'" Walker continued, wounding her regardless of the gentle voice he used. "That's a quote, Paige. He said, 'I'm not interested in her. I'm merely doing a good deed.'"

She could almost hear Matt say that. "A good deed," she repeated the words lamely.

Well, he'd done quite a "good deed" last night, hadn't he? And this morning. Yeah, that deed had been exceedingly good.

"And now I have to beat the you-know-what out of him," Walker added with enough of a smile to make it a joke.

"No, you don't," she said, hating the tears that filled her eyes. "He…he didn't want—" Didn't *want* to? Oh, he wanted to. But he didn't want Walker to know.

*I wish that your cousin won't kill me for seducing you.*

"He didn't seduce me."

Walker raked her with a look. "Obviously, he did."

"I initiated the encounter," she confessed boldly. "And I refuse to believe I was a charity case to him, literally or figuratively."

"Paige, you're too smart to be this stupid," Walker added, sliding his arm around her in a brotherly hug.

"Yeah, well, even smart people are entitled to their mistakes," she said, shrugging him off gently. "I'm making mine with my eyes wide open."

"Paige?" He looked oddly at her. "This isn't like you."

"No," she agreed with a false smile. "It isn't."

# Ten

Paige had to force herself to concentrate on what Detective Ryland was saying. Normally her keen analytical skills allowed her to block out everything, focus on the information in front of her, weigh it carefully and form an opinion.

But her razor-sharp mind had turned to mush.

And her body still hummed from Matt's lovemaking the night before.

And her heart? Under close observation and protection.

She took a sip of water and repositioned herself on the burgundy leather sofa where she sat between Megan and Trace.

"We're still tracking the money trail of the mysterious bank account Mr. Ashton had set up." Ryland directed his comments to Paige's mother, who perched straight-backed in a chair made for lounging.

But Lilah didn't lounge.

As the detective described the technology behind tracking the money trail for an account where, mysteriously, Spencer had deposited well over a million dollars during the past ten years, Paige studied her mother. Her deep-auburn hair curled softly under a chin that always remained tilted upward, as though the former secretary had studied the expected posture of a woman of means, then imitated it. For the most part, she kept her china-doll blue eyes trained on the detective, but occasionally glanced up at the family attorney, Stephen Cassidy, who stood protectively behind her.

In fact, she shared a good deal of message-filled glances with the man who'd supervised all of the Ashton's legal dealings for as long as Paige could remember. Lilah and Stephen seemed to communicate wordlessly.

Across the room, standing near his sister, Charlotte, and her husband, Alexandre Dupree, Walker leaned against one of the floor-to-ceiling bookshelves, a frown deepening a crease in his handsome forehead.

"Don't you have any new leads?" he asked, impatience coloring his tone.

Of course he was impatient. He hadn't flown in from South Dakota for a recap, Paige thought. Or just to plant seeds of doubt in Paige's heart.

Dan Ryland nodded. "That's why we're here, Mr. Ashton. As you know, several weeks ago a teenager admitted he'd been paid by a stranger to pick Grant Ashton out of a line up. In exchange for leniency, this young man agreed to help us create a sketch of the person who paid him."

Ryland's partner, a no-nonsense woman by the name of Nicole Holbrook, began distributing papers to everyone.

A palpable sense of hope filled the room as they all

studied the image intently, silently. A pencil drawing of a balding, beady-eyed man stared back at Paige, someone she'd guess was in his late forties. Someone, she'd hoped, who held the answer to the mystery of who murdered her father.

"Do you have any idea who this is?" Trace asked.

"We haven't yet made a positive identification," Ryland responded. "Although we have been running checks through various national law-enforcement databases. So far, there's no match to anyone who has ever been arrested or charged with a crime."

"There has to be some way to find out who this man is," Lilah insisted, her challenging glare locked on the detective. "This is taking entirely too long."

Stephen reached forward and laid a hand on her shoulder. "It does take time, Lilah," he said softly.

"And perhaps you can help," Detective Ryland added, obviously unaffected by Lilah's insinuation that they weren't doing enough.

"How?" Trace and Walker asked simultaneously.

"By sharing this photo with every employee of every Ashton business." This time he looked at Walker and Trace. "By searching any videotapes of winery tours, interviewing the security guards at the Ashton-Lattimer Company, reviewing any files that could contain photos of individuals who had business with the family, with Spencer or with any Ashton business."

"Isn't that your job?" Lilah demanded again.

"I'll get this sketch into the hands of everyone who works at Ashton-Lattimer," Walker offered, ignoring his aunt.

"And I'll get it through the winery," Trace agreed.

Ryland nodded. "Please run every cross-check you can."

"We maintain proof sheets of the photos taken at every event held at the winery," Megan said. "And almost every guest is captioned with a name."

"That's right," Paige nodded. "I'll go through the event photo files this afternoon." Although she seriously doubted the beady-eyed man had partied in the ballroom, it was a perfect diversion to keep her mind off the conversation with Walker…and the evening she had planned with Matt.

Stephen Cassidy looked hard at Detective Ryland. "Have you shared this with Caroline Sheppard's family?"

The detective shook his head. "Not yet. We will shortly." He glanced around the room at the other family members. "This is not necessarily a sketch of the murderer, but it is reasonable to assume this man has information about the crime."

"Or has a beef against Grant," Trace added.

"We've considered that option," the detective agreed. "We've got every available resource on the investigation."

As the detectives packed up, Walker cleared his throat and looked at Paige. "Can you stay here for a few minutes, Paige?"

Her heart dropped. Was he going to publicly chastise her for spending the night with his friend? She gave him a hard look, and he shook his head slightly as though he could read her mind. "We'd all like to hear about your trip to The Vines," he assured her.

Lilah escorted the two detectives into the foyer, where Irena showed them the door. When Paige's mother returned to the library, her shoulders seemed to sag ever so slightly. Stephen Cassidy put a comforting arm around her and led her across the library to a chair.

Next to Paige, Trace folded his arms behind his head

and blew out a frustrated breath. "They've got to find this guy."

"They're getting closer," Walker said. "And we'll do everything we can to help."

Lilah held up a hand to quiet them. "Now that we're all together, we need to discuss another issue." She spoke in general, but directed her attention to Paige. "What did you learn when you visited Louret, Paige? Is that woman still determined to contest your father's will?"

"That woman" would be Caroline Sheppard, but Paige bit back the correction. Lilah was loath to even acknowledge the existence of Spencer Ashton's previous wife, as they all knew from the way she'd treated Caroline's daughters when they'd shown up to make a sympathy call.

"To be honest, Mother, I don't think Caroline wants to pursue any legal action."

"That's a relief," Lilah said, with another knowing glance at Stephen.

"But Eli still does," Paige added.

Trace stifled a groan. "That guy's a loose cannon."

"I have had some informal conversations with their lawyers," Stephen announced. "They haven't made a decision yet regarding pursuing legal action, but they see it as two separate issues—contesting the will and contesting the divorce settlement."

Lilah paled, and Stephen's expression softened. "We'll handle this, Lilah," he promised.

Trace suddenly stood and dug his hands deep into the pockets of his pants. "There has to be a better way than long, drawn-out litigation."

Normally Paige would have jumped on that fair-minded concept, but she just stared ahead, hearing the words, but still thinking about the pronouncement Walker had made that morning.

*He's not interested in you. He was doing a good deed.*

Megan laid a gentle hand on Paige's arm. "You okay?" she whispered.

Paige gave her a quick nod and forced herself back to the present. "To be honest, they couldn't have been more accommodating when I visited," she told the group. "I was… impressed by their class."

Lilah bit back a decidedly unladylike snort, and Trace looked to the ceiling with a disgusted breath of disbelief.

As much as she longed for an end to the fighting between the half siblings, Paige had to admit that not all members of this family were ready for mending fences. And from what Jillian and Caroline had implied, neither were the men of the other family.

"I recommend we focus all efforts on helping the police find out who this man is," Stephen said, lifting a copy of the sketch from a desk. "Until this murder's solved, all the legal issues are moot."

For once, they all agreed.

By four o'clock Paige had looked at hundreds of pictures—hardcopy and digital—for a face that matched the sketch the police had shown them. Glancing at her watch, she decided to go through one more file before heading to her room for a good long soak and at least an hour of careful preparations.

*He really liked the black lace underwear,* she thought with a wicked smile. Maybe she'd wear red tonight.

Crackles of anticipation sparked through her as she opened the last file folder. And not because she thought she'd find the beady-eyed man.

She'd done an excellent job of silencing that nasty old voice of reason, as well as the even louder voice of her cousin Walker. Instead she'd just let the pleasant buzz of sexual tension sing through her veins all afternoon. She literally couldn't wait to get back to him. To kiss and touch and taste each other again.

A soft moan escaped her lips, and she forced herself to focus on the pictures in front of her.

And the first face she saw made her heart jump. It wasn't a match to the sketch, but a match to the man whose image danced around in her head.

Matthias Camberlane, the caption read, Attending the Annual Bachelorette Auction for the Candlelighters of Northern California. She'd forgotten his name was Matthias and not Matthew. Where did that name come from, she wondered, making a mental note to ask him later. In bed. Naked.

With a smile that couldn't be erased, she studied the picture, lingering on his handsome face, his steel-gray eyes, his fabulous six-foot-two-inch body encased in a very expensive suit.

Matthias Camberlane. Her *lover.*

The caption described him as A Self-Made Millionaire and Founder of Symphonics, Inc. Dropping her chin into her palms, she leaned forward and whispered, "Oh, but you're so much more than that, darling."

Slowly she turned the photo and discovered more captioned proofs that had been sent to the local papers. She skimmed the rows of pictures only halfheartedly searching for the beady-eyed target. In truth, she was looking for *gray* eyes. And chestnut-brown hair. And that sinfully talented mouth.

And there it was. That sinfully talented mouth smack-dab against the ear of…bachelorette number eleven, if memory served her right. The perky little brunette had one hand on his fabulous shoulder, the other draped possessively over that impressive chest.

Then she found him again. This time he had his arm around a statuesque blonde. Number four, Paige thought. Tara Something or Other from San Francisco.

And there was the good-looking self-made millionaire yet again. Flanked, in this photo, by a stunning set of redheaded twins. They'd gone for fifteen hundred apiece on a double-date special.

Paige slumped back in her chair.

*You're not his type, honey.* She could still hear Walker's voice. *He felt sorry for you.*

And, face it, Walker was right. Plain-brain Paige, the girl with hazel eyes and mouse-brown hair was not playing on the same field as these knockouts.

Torturing herself, Paige read the attached caption as it had been given to the photographer and then, the file noted, printed in the *San Francisco Chronicle* society column. "I can't believe I was outbid," Matt Camberlane stated. "I really wanted them both."

Her heart dropped into her stomach. And the voice of reason made a sudden, unscheduled appearance in her head.

*You're a fool, Paige Ashton. You were squirming under the lights and he was doing...a good deed.*

At the tap on her office door, Paige turned the photo facedown.

"Any luck, sweetie?" Megan asked.

Paige shook her head and closed the file. "Nope."

"Same in the winery. I've just been helping Trace's staff go through the records there. Nada." Megan gave her long, curious look. "Simon wants to get a bite in town and catch a movie. You want to join us tonight?"

Paige stared at her sister and waited for the voice of reason to holler out some advice.

One good deed deserves another.

"Yeah, Meg. I'd like that. I need to get my mind off…work."

He'd never been stood up before.

Matt stared at the keys of the Steinway, at the reflection of his fingers against the polished ebony of the piano dancing in what was left of the firelight.

He played the first few bittersweet notes of an old Cole Porter song, but swore when he missed a G-sharp.

Glancing at his cell phone—his extremely quiet cell phone—on top of the piano, he fought the urge to listen to Paige's voice mail message again.

Nah. Maybe he should belt down another shot of Scotch instead.

Disgusted, he pushed the bench out from underneath him and strode across the expanse of his living room, the sounds of the surf of Half Moon Bay drifting up the hilltop and through the open windows.

He'd gone for romance, all right. Wine, candles, fire, gourmet food and Ol' Blue Eyes on the invisible sound system that permeated every room.

Pouring that last shot he didn't want, Matt sank into a leather chair and set the glass down without drinking. He didn't need to listen to his voice mail because he'd memorized the message. She'd left it at four thirty-five; he'd been out on his lawn putting the final touches on a beach-view cocktail area for them and had left his cell phone in the kitchen.

Her voice had been tight but serious. No joke. No real apology, he noticed. Just a brief and businesslike cancellation.

"This is Paige Ashton," she'd said. As if he knew another Paige. "It looks like our family meeting is going to run well into the evening. So, I'll e-mail you all the follow-up from our meeting and will touch base with your assistant this week as the RSVPs start coming in. Thanks."

How *well* into the evening? Should he drive up there? Call her? Send flowers? Throw rocks at her bedroom window?

What the hell had happened to him? He had a crush, for God's sake. A stupid, massive, heart-crunching crush on a woman and…she'd stood him up.

He walked over to the piano and grabbed the cell phone. Not only had she stood him up—she'd done it by leaving a message. Something wasn't right. This just wasn't like Paige. Maybe something was wrong. Maybe…

He started to dial the Napa Valley area code then stopped, raking a hand through his hair. What was the matter with him?

Dropping onto the piano bench, he stared at the phone. What if something was wrong?

Something *was* wrong.

Paige was not here, not in his arms, not at his romantic little dinner on the patio and not in his bed. Where he wanted her. Tonight. And tomorrow. And the next night. And…

Jeez. He stabbed another cell number from memory into the phone.

"Yeah?" Walker answered on the first ring, impatience clear in his tone.

"Hey, Walker, it's Matt."

His friend didn't say anything for a minute, then gave a quick intake of breath. "What's the matter? Is Paige okay?"

Matt's chest tightened. "I'm not with Paige. I thought you were."

Walker laughed briefly. "Unless she's wandering around the Pine Ridge rez in South Dakota, she's not with me."

Matt blinked and held the phone away from his ear in disbelief. "Didn't your family meeting go, uh, well into the night?"

"I think you have been had, Matty boy," Walker said with a quick laugh. "Our meeting was over before lunch. I flew back this afternoon. To be with Tamra. A rendezvous, I might add, that you are interrupting."

"Sorry," Matt mumbled. "I guess she changed her mind."

"Or," Walker said quietly, "I might have changed it for her."

"What?"

"I caught her coming in this morning."

Matt swallowed, expecting the full fireworks from Walker. "Yeah, we, uh, got together last night."

"I figured."

"What did you say to her?"

Walker snorted softly. "I warned her, that's all. Same as I did you. But she's a grown woman, a fact that no doubt has caught your attention. I can't control my little cousin."

But evidently Walker *could* control her. Or at least convince her to stay away from him. "I really like her, Walker."

"I've seen what you do to women you like."

"I've never intentionally hurt anyone," he said defensively. "And I don't intend to hurt Paige."

All Matt could hear was the clean silence of their satellite connection. Then he thought he heard Tamra say something in the background.

"Hey, man, I didn't mean to interrupt. Apologies to Tamra."

"Listen, Matty," Walker said, after a moment of muffled conversation with his fiancée. "I told Paige you bid on her because you felt sorry for her."

"You did what?"

"It's the truth, isn't it?"

Regret rolled over him. Yeah, for one second, it had been the truth. And he'd even said that to Walker. But one look into those blue-green eyes. One conversation…one kiss…one unbelievable night…

"Walker," he said slowly, the truth of what he was about to admit hitting him hard. "This is different."

"Yeah." Walker could pack a whole bunch of cynicism into one syllable. "Prove it."

"Prove it?"

Then, for the first time in hours, Matt smiled.

There were few things in life he liked as much as a challenge.

# Eleven

**P**aige looked across the conference table at Matt, who was studying the song list she'd just presented to him. And as in every other meeting they'd had during the past three weeks—and there had been plenty—her empty stomach tightened.

*Empty* because he always managed to arrange their meetings near lunchtime. Or dinner. And the occasional breakfast.

So they weren't technically dates, those long lunches and dinners that just naturally occurred after their meetings. They were just two business associates …sharing stories and easy laughs. They always included notebooks and agendas and items for discussion.

Even though they discussed family—his and hers—as much as work. And their childhoods. And their dreams. And their favorite songs, books and movies.

But never once did those "meetings" include a mention of the night they'd made love, or the dinner date at his house that never happened.

That was why her stomach—empty or otherwise—tightened. That and the fact that just looking at him made her ache. Listening to him made her weak. And working side by side on every minor detail of the Voice-Box launch party just made her...happy. There was no other word for it.

Well, there was. But it wasn't a word she dared use when she thought about Matt Camberlane. Which was just about every minute of every day.

"I don't see much country on here," he commented, looking up at her with those tantalizing gray eyes. "Didn't someone say they are coming as Faith Hill and Tim McGraw?"

She frowned. "I know we've programmed in a bunch of Garth Brooks, but I'll check with the sound man tomorrow. There's still time."

But not much. The event was three days away, and this late-Friday-afternoon meeting at his office was one of her last legitimate opportunities to be with Matt. After this, their business was over. The thought made her throat swell, and she forced the lump away.

He'd done his good deed, and she'd done one right back by coordinating a killer event. They were square.

It wasn't his fault she'd gone and fallen in love with him in the process.

He put the song sheet away and picked up the next item: the final menu.

"I made some last-minute changes to the appetizers," she commented, gnawing her lip as her gaze took a leisurely trip over the snug fit of his blue oxford shirt. Those arms had held her all night one time.

Would he ever hold her again?

Not likely. And heaven knew he'd had enough opportunities since the day she'd canceled their dinner date.

But he'd been nothing but a perfect gentleman. Warm, friendly, professional. He listened and talked and made her laugh, he advised and shared his opinions and congratulated her on every great idea.

But he never, ever kissed her again.

He slapped the menu on his conference table and grinned. "That made me hungry. Want to try Ellsworth again tonight?"

They'd visited the stylish restaurant in downtown San Mateo twice already. Both times, they'd shared a corner booth and a wild mushroom tart.

Like good friends.

"I don't want to."

He gave her a surprised look. "No? It's almost six o'clock. But you're right, that place gets pretty ridiculous on a Friday night. Want to go somewhere quieter?"

Yes. Your house. And I want to stay until tomorrow.

Her reasonable voice, thank God, answered for her. "Actually, Matt, I have to get back home. There's so much to prepare for the party on Monday night and—"

He reached over and laid his hand over hers, the warmth from his fingertips searing her skin. "Don't worry, Paige. The party's going to be great."

"I'm not worried," she countered.

"You seem…distracted."

Distracted? She was wildly, madly, hopelessly in love. Yeah, that could be a little distracting. But she just stared at him, searching his handsome face for a crack in that platonic demeanor he'd worn for the past few weeks.

"I'm fine," she lied. "I just want to be sure the Voice-Box party is flawless."

He squeezed her hand. "You've done an amazing job. I'm not worried about a thing."

Easing her hand out from his touch, she started to pack up her papers. "Megan always says it's not the ten things you expect to go wrong, it's the one you never dreamed of."

She could feel his eyes on her, and that just made her pulse kick into high gear.

"Then let's dream."

Her hands froze over the papers, and she lifted her eyes to meet his. "About what?"

"About what could go wrong," he said as though there couldn't be anything else in the world for them to dream about.

"Oh, I don't know…a power outage, the chef breaks his arm, nobody shows up." *You shake my hand good-night and walk out of my life forever.* "There are lots of potential heartaches, er, mistakes that could happen."

For what seemed like an eternity he studied her, and she managed to look right back but couldn't read the message in his eyes. "Whatever happens, Paige," he said so slowly the very air she breathed threatened to strangle her. "It's been a pleasure working with you."

She tried, but failed, to swallow. A *pleasure*. It had been. Once. Well, several times that night. "This has been a fun project," she managed.

"I've learned a lot," he said, the serious tone in his voice catching her attention.

"Like what?"

He just laughed softly. "I'll tell you when it's all over," he said. "We'll have a formal debriefing."

Well, at least that meant one more meeting. Formal or otherwise.

Gathering up all her strength and listening to the voice of reason instead of the one that screamed, *Kiss him, kiss him, kiss him,* she stood and scooped up her portfolio.

"I'll see you Monday."

Before he could talk her out of that, she managed to rush out the door, praying that she could drive all the way home with the tears that were about to make an appearance.

The pounding bass of the sound system literally shook the floor of Paige's office, which was directly above the ballroom. Through the open windows of the solarium, she could hear the familiar buzz of a party floating on the evening air: music, laughter, conversation and the clink of crystal glasses.

She should be down there. She should be checking the kitchen, supervising the waitstaff, watching for problems.

Instead, she'd escaped. She'd avoided anything but the most necessary contact with Matt, spending at least fifteen minutes of every hour up here attending to some very important business.

The business of licking her wounds and easing the excruciating ache in her heart. And the occasional self-chastising for being such a stupid fool for falling for Matt. Yes, she was very busy indeed.

At the sound of her door latch clicking, she tensed but didn't step out of the sunroom to see who was there.

She waited, hoping against hope to hear that baritone voice. Was it possible he'd come up in search of her? To finally admit that he—

"Paige?"

Walker.

She blew out a breath of pure self-disgust. Matt Camberlane, chief executive chick magnet, was probably dancing with Tessa Carpenter from his Marketing Department right now, laughing at her uncanny resemblance to Shania Twain and twirling his Frank Sinatra felt hat.

"Paige? Are you in here?"

"In the sunroom, Walker," she called out.

Walker's giant frame filled the doorway in an instant. "Why aren't you downstairs?"

She threw him a "get real" look, then covered it with her own question. "Why didn't you come in costume?"

"You didn't," he countered, glancing at the simple black cocktail dress she wore.

"I'm working."

"So am I."

She raised an eyebrow. "Doing what?"

"Supervising my little cousin," he said with a teasing glint in his dark eyes.

"You have nothing to worry about, Walker. Nothing to supervise. Matt has been a perfect gentlemen." Unfortunately. "There's nothing going on between us."

"I wouldn't say that."

She crossed her arms and turned toward the window. "You're wrong. He's become a friend, that's all."

"How good a friend?"

She closed her eyes. "Please. He hasn't laid a hand on me. He's been…wonderful. We work together like a well-oiled team, he makes me laugh, he gives me advice, he listens and talks and, oh…" There were the tears again. She looked up at her cousin and finally said it. "I'm completely in love with him."

In an instant Walker put his arm around her. "Yeah, I saw that."

She shook her head. "Great. It's obvious, huh?"

"Actually, I noticed that he was in love with you."

A thrill zipped through Paige, but she wisely tamped it down before it took hold of her heart. "You've mistaken friendship and fondness for love."

"I don't know about that." He squeezed her affectionately. "I've known Matty a long time. I've never seen him quite like this."

She looked up at him. "Like what?"

He grinned. "Tamed."

*Tamed?*

"Come to the party," Walker said. "Lots of people— one in particular—miss you down there."

His voice was rich with meaning, and Paige studied him closely to decipher it.

Could he be right?

Matt stood to the side of the stage, nursing a drink that had long ago lost its taste. He pretended to watch his head of Human Resources dressed as Aretha Franklin belt out "Respect" but mostly he was scanning the entrances for the beautiful woman in a slinky black dress who'd left a few minutes ago.

With no warning, Walker was suddenly behind him. Matt was about to make a joke about his natural Native American stealth, when Walker said, "Paige is in her office."

"What's she doing up there?" he asked.

"Nursing a broken heart."

Matt put the drink down on the stage floor and turned to Walker, denial spurting through his veins. "I haven't—"

"I know." Walker held up a hand and smiled. "She told me you haven't."

For a moment the two men just stared at each other.

"You told me to prove she's different," Matt said. "She is. And I did."

Walker nodded, but held Matt's gaze. "You always surprise me, Matty boy. So now what?"

Matt grinned and put a friendly hand on Walker's shoulder. "More surprises, Walker."

"Aretha Franklin" finished her song with a flourish and the applause stopped their conversation.

"And now, ladies and gentlemen," she announced to the crowd. "By popular demand, our very own CEO, Matt Camberlane has agreed to play."

"He can't sing!" A guy in the crowd yelled out.

"That's for sure," Matt said with a laugh as he took the stairs two at a time and stepped into the lights. "But I can play."

As the crowd quieted down, he sat at the piano and stretched his fingers. The lights blinded all but the front tables.

That's where he had sat the night he'd bid on Paige. Had she been able to see the look on his face the first time he saw her? And couldn't she see that same look every time they were together?

Ten thousand dollars for a date? Hah. He'd have paid a hundred thousand for the contentment and happiness he felt around her. No matter what the cost, he wanted Paige. Then and now.

And now he wanted more than the fleeting moments of contentment and happiness she gave him. He wanted it all. A lifetime of it.

His fingers settled into the familiar opening chords of "I've Got You Under My Skin."

Man, did he ever have that woman under his skin.

He finished the first verse and looked back into the lights. And almost missed a note to a song he'd played a thousand times.

She stood near the stage, her great big eyes trained on him, her lips mouthing the words. Backlit by the spotlight, the honey streaks in her hair looked dazzling, like a halo.

He tilted his head in invitation. "Sing for me," he mouthed to her.

A sweet smile was all he got in response. God, he loved her. He cocked his head again. "Come on."

"I'm working." She glanced at the crowd. "I can't."

"Can't?" He raised an eyebrow and whispered, "I don't know what that word means."

Behind her, he saw Walker say something in her ear and she laughed softly. Then, son of a gun, she started toward the stage.

When she sat down next to him, she caught his gaze and held it. Taking the microphone from the stand, she waited for him to start the second verse, and then she sang. For the next two verses, they never took their eyes off each other until he hit the final chord.

Then he moved his hands from the keyboard, slid his fingers over her creamy skin and lifted her face to his.

"You were right," he whispered. "It's not the ten things you expect. It's the one you never dreamed could happen."

And then he kissed her the way he'd been dying to for weeks.

# Twelve

It was well past midnight when the last of the staff left the kitchen and Paige was ready to lock up the ballroom. There was only one person left.

Matt. Who'd been playing a medley on the piano for the last hour, patiently waiting for her.

She kicked off her heels and tiptoed up the stage steps. His eyes were closed as he played something soft and romantic, his jacket long ago discarded.

She stood behind him, then slowly slid her arms around his chest and leaned to whisper in his ear. "The party's over."

"No way, sweetheart." He turned and gave her a provocative grin. "It's just about to start."

A blast of heat whipped through her. "Don't tell me you want to have that debriefing now."

"As a matter of fact—" he stood and turned to hold her in his arms "—I do."

"You are one demanding client," she laughed.

"You have no idea."

The words sent more heat lightning shooting to every female cell in her body.

"What did you have in mind?" she asked, snuggling closer.

"I'm staying at Auberge tonight." He dipped his head to place his lips against her ear. "With you."

An hour later they arrived in his suite. A bucket of chilled champagne waited by the fireplace, which had been lit. A late, light supper had been recently delivered by room service. Music filled the room, and the bed, of course, had been turned back.

Before they'd left, she'd packed a small overnight bag, which he unobtrusively put in the bedroom while Paige strolled around and took in the ambiance of the living area.

"You planned this," she said with a note of teasing accusation when he returned.

"For a long time."

"Excuse me?"

"Since you unceremoniously dumped me with a voice mail."

"Matt—"

He placed a finger on her lips and shushed her. "You did the right thing."

"It sure didn't feel like the right thing."

He slid his arms around her and pulled her closer. "But it does now." Guiding her over to the intimate dinner setting, he eased her onto the chaise next to it. "I watched you all night. You didn't eat tonight."

"I was too busy." And too much in love.

He handed her a silver bowl of calamata olives.

"Please. Be an angel and let me watch you torture an innocent olive."

She giggled a little and took one. "Mmm," she moaned as she took a bite.

Before she swallowed, he bent over her and kissed her, taking the olive right from her mouth. Blood coursed through her as he turned the shared bite into a heated kiss.

"Oh," she said a little breathlessly when he pulled away. "That was torture."

He laughed as he uncorked the champagne. "You were amazing tonight," he said, nestling next to her. "That was the best launch party—the best *party*—I've ever been to."

Taking the glass he offered, she thanked him with a smile. "It's easy when you like your client."

"Oh, yeah? What do you like about him?"

"Everything."

He touched her crystal flute with his. "Then we both succeeded at our goals. To success."

Bubbles tingled against her lips as she sipped. "So, what was your goal?"

His gaze dropped to the deep V of her dress. Leaning over her, he tilted his champagne glass just enough to let a single drop fall against the rise of her breast.

Then he lowered his head and licked it off. Paige moaned softly as his tongue burned hot against the cold liquid, fighting the urge to sink back into the chaise and let him lick every inch of her just that way.

"My goal," he said, taking her glass and putting it with his on the table. "Is to drive you crazy."

"You did that weeks ago," she assured him. "And that olive thing you just did was pretty, uh, crazy."

He leaned into her and kissed her. "I haven't even started to get crazy," he promised as he broke away from her mouth. "But first," he whispered, "I am going to make you dizzy."

True to his word, his hand slid under her skirt and his fingers grazed her inner thigh as he burned a trail on her skin. She closed her eyes, definitely dizzy.

He kissed her again, delving his tongue deep into her mouth, then feathering soft kisses against her cheek, her jaw, down her throat.

Very slowly he turned her so he could unzip her dress. More kisses against her skin. With two hands he guided the straps over her shoulders and then he let out a soft moan.

"Do you know," he spoke into her ear, his voice like a baritone instrument as beautiful as the music he played. "How many times I imagined doing this while we were…meeting?"

"About as many as I have."

With her back still to him, she slipped out of the dress, wearing nothing back a whisper of black panties, then dropped her head against his chest to offer him the flesh of her neck, which he suckled. His hands curled around to fondle her breasts, sending shockwaves at the heated contact. Turning to face him, she easily repositioned them on the chaise so Matt lay back, then she climbed on top of him. Slowly she unbuttoned his shirt.

A declaration of love screamed in her head, but she managed to contain it, focusing on each new angle of his chest and stomach as she undressed him.

Leaning against him, she whispered his name, loving the feel of his masculine hair against her bare breasts. Loving the strength of his muscles, the single-minded desire that came off him in waves.

"We've been here before," she said quietly, tapping the silky fabric of the chaise behind his head.

He became perfectly still, a sadness suddenly changing his expression. "I'm sorry I made you cry."

"No." She shook her head, leaning up on her elbows but keeping their skin in contact. "I made myself cry. I was just overwhelmed that someone like you would be...interested in someone like me."

He closed his eyes as though the comment cut right through him. "You're kidding, right? How about that someone like you—classy and smart and raised in a mansion—would be interested in someone like me?"

This time she quieted him with a kiss. "I'm more than interested, Matt. I'm...crazy...about you."

"See? Success," he said with a teasing laugh.

Holding his gaze, she sat up to unbuckle his belt and unfasten his pants. While she did, he caressed her breasts and ran his hands down her waist and over her backside.

When she closed her fingers over the swell of his manhood, he gritted his teeth and sucked in air.

He moved against her hand, sending a surge of power and delight through Paige. She loved that he wanted her as much as she wanted him.

They finished undressing and then she pushed him back on the chaise. Straddling him, then sliding on a condom he gave her, she arched her back and he caressed and kissed her breasts, her mouth, her face and throat.

"Let me love you, Paige," he whispered, the head of his erection throbbing against her opening. "Let me love you."

She lifted her hips and slowly guided him into her.

As he entered her, they both gasped. She could have sworn his eyes were moist, but beads of sweat had built up on his temples and she tasted the salt when she kissed his cheeks and neck.

He closed his eyes and mouthed her name and filled her completely. Slowly, easily, he moved in and out, increasing the intensity with each thrust.

Clinging to his powerful arms, she encircled his hips with her legs, and tilted to get him even deeper, wanting to scream with the complete happiness of this union.

She closed her eyes as the waves of an orgasm started, carrying her one after another, closer and closer, unable to stop as the sweet ache made her arch above him.

Lost in his own response, he gripped her hips and drove harder and harder into her. His chest and arm muscles flexed with the effort to control himself, and rivulets of sweat trickled over his cheeks and neck. Finally he gave in. With a low, long groan of satisfaction, he thrust himself as deep as he could go and let the release overtake him.

She clung to his shoulders, gently rocking him as their hearts hammered in unison.

When she lifted her head and looked at him, streaks of sweat were still sliding over the stubble on his cheeks. She touched his mouth, his cheeks, his eyelids. And then realized that the moisture wasn't sweat and it had come from his eyes.

"Matt?" she said tentatively.

He managed a bittersweet smile. "Must be this chaise," he said softly. "It just gets us every time."

Paige's cell phone rang just as Matt parked his car near Ghirardelli Square late the next morning.

"I'll bet it's Megan," Paige said. "I'm sure she wants to know where the heck I am." As she answered the phone, she nodded to him and, rolling her eyes, greeted her sister.

"I'm fine, Meg. I just decided to…" A slow smile tipped her lips. A smile just for him.

"We're just celebrating our success." She spoke into the phone, but winked at Matt. "I'm in San Francisco. Nothing to worry about."

He liked that her family checked on her. For all their issues, for all their gossip-generating activities and ancient secrets and unsolved mysteries, there was a foundation of love among all the Ashtons that couldn't be denied. It made him a little envious.

More than that, it made him want to be part of it.

"She says hi." Paige announced as she snapped the phone closed.

He grinned. "Here, give me your phone." Taking it, he opened it up and started stabbing buttons.

"What are you doing?"

"Programming my ring. When I call you, you'll know it's me." After a minute, he held it back to her with a triumphant look. "Listen."

The opening notes of "I've Got You Under My Skin" beeped a digital melody.

"You'll know it's me whenever you hear it."

She looked pleasantly surprised. "Are you planning to call me a lot?"

"Is three times a day a lot?"

That made her laugh, but he could tell she didn't believe him. That was fine. It might be four times a day, anyway.

"Okay, we have a very important errand to do here," he announced as they got out of the car.

"We do?" She smoothed the jeans she'd changed into and slid her arm around his waist. He liked her there, tucked under his arm.

That's where she had to be. Always.

His gut constricted just a little. Not from fear. Not from misgivings or trepidation. He knew what he wanted. He just hoped she wanted it, too.

"Where are we going?" she asked.

"We need to visit an old friend."

She glanced up at him questioningly but didn't ask for specifics.

They had another gorgeous day. The sky was that heartbreak blue that God saved for California, and the air was crisp and clean. The scent of chocolate mixed with the salty smell of the Bay as they walked arm in arm amidst swarms of tourists and visitors.

In a few minutes they arrived at the fountain.

"Ah," she said knowingly, "Andrea."

He nodded. "She worked so well last time, I thought we ought to give her another shot."

She poked him playfully in the ribs. "All I wanted was one kiss, and look what I got. You were right—be careful what you wish for."

Taking her hand, he guided her over to the stone steps that surrounded the fountain, the light spray of water cooling them as it got caught in the wind.

"You never told me what you wished for that day, Matt."

He peered at the splashing water and considered his answer. He'd wished to win his bet. For his brain to be smarter than his body.

And, son of a gun, the brain had trounced the body. And everybody won. "I got my wish," he said simply.

From his pocket, he pulled out some change and opened his hand. As she reached for a penny, he snapped his hand shut, making her giggle.

"Wait," he said. "I'm first."

She gave him a surprised look, then shrugged. "Okay."

"I only have a penny," he said, holding it up between his two fingers.

"So don't go for anything too serious like a lifetime of contentment and happiness," she warned him.

He tossed the coin, watching it flip end over end until it landed with a soft splash. "Funny, a lifetime of contentment and happiness is exactly what I wished for."

Then he reached into his other pocket, but she was looking into his eyes. When he opened his hand, she looked down.

And said nothing.

His heart thumped and somewhere in the distance a seagull squawked, but all he heard was the blood rushing in his ears as he waited for that gorgeous, wide-eyed, blue-green gaze to meet his.

Finally it did. Moist with tears and glinting with happiness. "That's no penny, Matt."

He grinned. "It's lucky, though. I promise."

With his other hand, he took the diamond ring and held it, like the penny, between his two fingers. "I have one wish, Paige Ashton. And that's to spend the rest of my life making wishes with you."

She tried to swallow a lump that must have felt just as big as the stupid one in his throat.

She opened her mouth to speak, but nothing came out. Then she blinked and a tear slid down her cheek. "That is some serious *string* for a sex-without-stings kind of guy."

He choked out a laugh. "I think I forgot something important here."

He dropped to one knee and took her hand, his eyes never leaving hers. "I love you, Paige. I've never met anyone as precious and perfect and sweet and smart and wonderful as you are. I love you because you've changed me and made me want to be tied up in so many strings that I can't breathe." He slid the ring onto her shaking finger. "Paige, will you marry me and make me the luckiest guy in the world?"

She tried to laugh, but it came out a sob, her lips shuddering as she fought the emotion. "I love you, too, Matt. I don't know what to say."

"You don't?" He gave her an incredulous look as he slowly stood back up. "Say *yes*."

"Yes!" She threw her arms around him, and he twirled her in a circle so wildly that they sent a flock the pigeons squealing into the sky. And when he kissed her, all the tourists in Ghirardelli Square burst into applause.

It was the most beautiful music Matt had ever heard.

\* \* \* \* \*

*Look for the next installment of*
DYNASTIES: THE ASHTONS,
*Laura Wright's SAVOR THE SEDUCTION,
available in November from Silhouette Desire.*

**Coming in November
from Silhouette Desire**

# DYNASTIES: THE ASHTONS

*A family built on lies...brought together
by dark, passionate secrets*

**continues with**

## SAVOR THE SEDUCTION

## by Laura Wright

Grant Ashton came
to Napa Valley to discover the truth
about his family...but found so much
more. Was Anna Sheridan, a woman
battling her own demons, the answer
to all Grant's desires?

*Available this November wherever
Silhouette books are sold.*

A violent storm.

A warm cabin.

One bed…for two strangers
stranded overnight.

Author

# Bronwyn Jameson's

latest PRINCES OF THE OUTBACK novel
will sweep you off your feet and into
a world of privilege and passion!

Don't miss

# The Ruthless Groom

Silhouette Desire #1691
Available November 2005

Only from Silhouette Books!

**Silhouette**

*Desire*

# COMING NEXT MONTH

**#1687 SAVOR THE SEDUCTION—Laura Wright**
*Dynasties: The Ashtons*
Scandals had rocked his family but only one woman was able to shake him to the core.

**#1688 BOSS MAN—Diana Palmer**
*Long, Tall Texans*
This tough-as-leather attorney never looked twice at his dedicated assistant…until now!

**#1689 HIGHLY COMPROMISED POSITION—Sara Orwig**
*Texas Cattleman's Club: The Secret Diary*
How could she have known the sexy stranger who fathered her child was her family's sworn enemy?

**#1690 THE CHASE IS ON—Brenda Jackson**
*The Westmorelands*
His lovely new neighbor was a sweet temptation this confirmed bachelor couldn't resist.

**#1691 THE RUTHLESS GROOM—Bronwyn Jameson**
*Princes of the Outback*
She delivered the news that his bride-to-be had run away…never expecting to be next on his "to wed" list.

**#1692 MISTLETOE MANEUVERS—Margaret Alison**
Mixing business with pleasure could only lead to a hostile takeover…and a whole lot of passion.

SDCNM1005